The Short Story Series

GENERAL EDITOR   JAMES GIBSON

ADVENTURE
ANIMAL
DETECTION
HORROR
HUMOUR
LOVE
SCIENCE FICTION
SEA
SPORT
SUPERNATURAL
TRAVEL
WESTERN

Western

CHOSEN BY
F. E. S. Finn

John Murray

Albemarle Street London

Printed and bound in Great Britain
by Butler & Tanner Ltd,
Frome and London

0 7195 3667 7

CONTENTS

Mountain Skill, Mountain Luck by Winfred
   Blevins   1

The Shaming of Broken Horn by Bill Gulick   19

The Guns of William Longley by Donald
   Hamilton   34

The Man Who Knew the Buckskin Kid by
   Dorothy M. Johnson   48

Blanket Squaw by Dorothy M. Johnson   60

The Gift of Cochise by Louis L'Amour   76

Trap of Gold by Louis L'Amour   90

Emmet Dutrow by Jack Schaefer   98

In the Silence by Peggy S. Curry   112

Acknowledgements   120

Winfred Blevins

Mountain Skill, Mountain Luck

The story of Hugh Glass sounds like some yarn spun by a veteran and carried all over the plains by some green listeners who told it without understanding the game. Maybe part of the story is a yarn, the part before old Glass met up with a grizzly in South Dakota one September morning. After that, it has a lot of wise hands to vouch for it. And it was too good for even mountain men to improve on.

Glass is said to have been a sailor, perhaps even an officer, working in the Caribbean in the years just after the war with the British. In 1817, he had the bad luck to encounter Jean Lafitte, the pirate who saved Andrew Jackson at New Orleans and then returned to piracy. Lafitte captured Glass's ship and its crew. He gave Glass the choice of becoming a pirate or being dispatched instantly to another world. Glass made the prudent choice, and was taken to Lafitte's current lair, Galveston Island. After perhaps a year of pirating, Glass could stand it no longer, rebelled at doing something especially repulsive, and was told he would be executed. With a friend, he decided to swim for it. Their chief worry was cannibalistic Indians over on the mainland. But if they could stay hidden and work their way northeast, they could join an outpost of Americans in Texas near the Louisiana border.

They swam and managed to escape the Karankawas, but, somehow, they managed to misread the sun enough to travel more northwest than northeast. Instead of getting to Louisiana, they ended up in western Kansas, in Pawnee Country. The Pawnees captured the two and promptly made a human sacrifice of Glass's friend. As Glass was about to help placate the Pawnee gods as well, he handed the Pawnee chief some vermilion. The impressionable fellow was so taken with this gift that he not only spared Hugh's life, but adopted him as a son.

So, in 1818 or 1819, Glass became a Pawnee and began to master plains craft as he had mastered marine craft. At some later time, his adopted father made a journey to St Louis, to see William Clark, now Superintendent of Indian Affairs. Hugh went along, and, in St Louis, he again became a white man.

Perhaps Hugh's story is fanciful to this point. But from here on, it is well substantiated and even more fabulous.

In the spring of 1823, Glass enlisted with the Ashley-Henry men who were going up the Missouri River to trap in the mountains. General Ashley, an important political figure in the new state of Missouri, had already sent brigades to the mountains last year, and St Louis was aflurry with reports that these men were going to bring back a fortune greater than the wealth of the mines of Peru. People said that any man who was enterprising, didn't mind a little hardship, and didn't quail at danger, ought to have a try. Glass, who had been a wanderer and adventurer on the seas, had fallen for the plains and decided to have a go with Ashley.

Ashley led the band upriver to the Arikara villages, where they were attacked by this unpredictable tribe, and forced back down. Fifteen men were killed in the battle, and Hugh was wounded in the leg. It was the worst defeat any American trappers had suffered to date. Ashley realized that he had to take some action to keep the river route to the Stony Mountains open; the Arikaras would be even more dangerous after this heady victory. So he secured the help, not only of the rival fur company, but of the US Army. These Rees (as the Arikaras were also called) must be made to know their place.

Unfortunately, the commander of the expedition against the Rees, Colonel Leavenworth, turned the affair into a comic opera of miscalculations. He let the Rees get away scot-free, so they were not chastened but aroused and encouraged to thumb their noses at the ineffective white men.

Ashley and his field leader, Major Andrew Henry, led their men downriver in great discouragement. The river route was now closed. They had to get to the mountains, and their only choice was a land expedition. At Fort Kiowa they scrounged up a few horses—not enough so that the men could ride, but enough to get the supplies to Fort Henry at the mouth of the Yellowstone. Major Henry would lead one small land party, very carefully. The Rees had disappeared after the farcical campaign against them; no one knew where they were, and now would not be a good time to find out by accident.

Henry's party of thirteen left Fort Kiowa in mid-August, moving up the Missouri and then due west up the Grand River. The plains of South Dakota were scrubby, nearly barren, flat, dry, unaccommodating. Henry put men out ahead and to the side to watch for buffalo and for Rees. But on one of the first few nights, an Indian attack left two men dead and two more wounded.

Glass was not a leader in the party. He was a new man, relatively speaking, and the party counted on veterans like Black Harris and Hiram Allen. So, five days and probably a couple of hundred miles out of Fort Kiowa, two old hands were ahead of the main party, hunting. Glass, at about forty, had been his own master too long to traipse along docilely with the others. He liked to be by himself, and he was as stubborn, insubordinate, and independent as any mountain man. He was out ahead, against discipline, looking for some berries, when he stumbled into a thicket and onto a huge grizzly and her two cubs.

Old Ephraim charged, and Hugh knew what he was in for. He didn't take off running because he knew where his best chance lay. When the grizzly reached him, she stopped long enough to raise up on her hind legs so that she could swat him with her forepaws. Hugh waited, shoved his fear out of the way of his vision, and, when she exposed her chest, shot directly at her heart. Then he dropped his gun and ran desperately, screaming for help at the top of his lungs. (The rifles of the mountain men, unfortunately, fired just once. Then it took thirty seconds to get more powder and another ball in place.)

The grizzly caught Hugh after a dozen or two steps and with one swipe sent him sprawling. Then she hit the limp body again. Then she tore off a piece of flesh and carried it back to her cubs.

Black Harris was the first to get there. When he burst into the thicket, one of the cubs took after him and chased him into the river. From chest-deep water Harris shot and killed the cub. The rest of the party ran towards the snarling she-grizzly. They found Glass gamely slashing at her with his knife, but she was mangling him with every swat. When she knocked him down and started to pounce on him again, several men fired balls into her. Finally, from Hugh's original shot, or from the new shots, she keeled over next to Glass's body.

When they turned Glass over, they were surprised to find him breathing at all. His face was partly raked away to the bones. His ribs were crushed. An awful tear in his throat bubbled every time he breathed. His body was littered with gashes. Any one of fifteen wounds was enough to kill him. The men smiled a little, sadly, but admiringly, at the gumption of a man who could live even for a few minutes after having gotten so torn up. They hovered, waiting for the old man to die. After a few minutes, they decided to make camp. After the burying, there wouldn't be time to move that day, anyway. Strangely, when dark came and they turned in, old Glass was still hanging on.

And in the morning he was still hanging on. Now the whole thing was beginning to get embarrassing. For Glass to live a little while was touching, but for him to survive the night was dangerous.

Henry did what he had to do. The Rees could be anywhere, and it was essential to get out of their territory as quickly as possible. It made absolutely no sense to risk ten lives waiting for another man to die so that they could go through some ritual of duty. The men were already antsy. But, still, Henry could not bring himself to abandon a man who still clung to life. That was something a decent man just didn't do. So he compromised. He asked for two volunteers to stay with Glass until the old man gave up, bury him, and hightail it after the main party.

Right off the kid volunteered, a gangly nineteen-year-old of no particular account named Jim Bridger. This wasn't the sort of man you left almost alone in a hostile country. Henry looked at the other men. He was an old hand at the mountains and at leading men, so he didn't berate them. He just told them that the job had to be done, and asked who was willing to do it. John Fitzgerald spoke up. It wasn't fair, he said. A man would be daring the Rees to take his scalp, would get nothing done with the dare, and would get nothing for his trouble in the end. Might even come out behind, 'cause he might miss the fall hunt if he couldn't get to the fort quick enough. Maybe, if Henry made it worth a man's while. . . .

At least Fitzgerald had been around a little. Maybe he could get this boy back with all his hair on his head. Henry declared the company would go forty dollars a man to stay behind, if Fitzgerald would stay. Fitzgerald allowed that he would. Forty dollars was two or three months' pay.

They broke camp quickly, all of them fidgety about having hung around so long and uneasy about making their way to the mouth of the Yellowstone with just the eight men left. Henry noticed young Bridger standing around self-consciously straight, like he thought everyone was looking at him. Henry had a nagging feeling that Bridger might pay dearly for his chance to look good. He shrugged the feeling off. In this situation he couldn't afford it. They cleared out.

Bridger didn't really pay any mind to Fitzgerald or the mauled body he was guarding for an hour or two. He sat and stared at his rifle, his mind back home in Missouri where he had been bonded to a blacksmith and hated the life. He imagined the surprise and envy in the blacksmith's eyes if he could see his bound boy now. He remembered when, slaving on his folks' farm on the river above St Louis, he had watched the keelboats headed upriver, into wilderness country, where a man might show that he could do brave things, the kind of things that other men told stories about. He had longed, at twelve, to go up one of the two great rivers with those men and be one of them. He smiled to himself.

He needed a moment to take in that Fitzgerald was talking to him. 'I'm gonna have a look around,' he said. 'Why don't you see what you can do for him?'

'Do for him.' It hadn't quite struck Bridger that they would have to do for old Glass until he went under. He guessed they would. They had to give him his fair chance, even if he didn't have none. He stood over the body and looked down at it. It looked peaceful, asleep, and maybe resting. Bridger looked at the awful wounds, half bound with strips of Glass's dirty shirt but still showing raw for all that. He felt a little nauseated. He picked a piece of rag from the shirt lying next to Glass, stepped over to the spring to soak it, and poked it into Glass's open mouth. Glass's eyelids fluttered a little, and he sucked on the rag. Well, they would just wait, that's all. At least they had water without even going the twenty steps to the creek, and enough dried meat without having to shoot and make a ruckus that could be heard. There were even buffler berries for a change, if they wanted one. He wondered where Fitzgerald was. He himself wouldn't even have left the thicket to check for Rees. They had all they needed right here and could sit tight and not be seen till the job was done.

The mouth had stopped sucking, he noticed, and he reached out for the rag. Fitzgerald spoke before Bridger saw him standing behind. 'How's his breathing?'

Bridger felt around the nose and mouth for the air. 'Feeble,' he answered. 'And fitful.'

It seemed callous to say more, but Fitzgerald did. 'Won't be long then, and it's a good thing. This country makes a man uncomfortable alone.'

Bridger felt a twinge of resentment. Fitzgerald wasn't alone, was he? He walked over and got a handful of berries, crushed them, and put them in Glass's mouth one by one. He wasn't afraid to stick the job out. Fitzgerald sat and waited, not paying any mind to Bridger or Glass. Bridger could sense that Fitzgerald's sitting was uneasy.

They got into their buffalo robes early that night, since they couldn't build a fire. Bridger wished to hell Fitzgerald would say something—just anything, just talk, to show that they were two human beings and not something else. He forgot: three human beings, though one couldn't talk and wasn't any company. He guessed Glass would be gone by morning. Bridger had seen more than a few dead men, since he'd been in the mountains a year and a half. So that didn't bother him. He turned his head and peered through the darkness toward the black shape, no more than ten feet away. It was a funny notion, the idea of sleeping practically next to a body that might be alive and might be dead.

Come morning, Glass was still alive. Fitzgerald checked him and said that the fever had come up to him and he wouldn't stand against it long. If the tearing up and the losing blood didn't get him, the fever would take him off pretty quick. Bridger was ashamed of it, but he felt a little relieved. Why, what if old Glass held out for a couple of weeks? What could they do about that?

He took his turn walking out to check around that day, going slow and quiet and turning himself into all eyes and all ears. This country wasn't fat, like the upper Missouri country, at least not this time of year. It was decidedly thin. The sun had dried the sandy soil almost into a crust, like it had been in an oven. Sun and wind had got the sagebrush and the cottonwoods crackling dry, and had turned what little green there was to grey. The Dakota country swept away in scrubby hills as far as he could see, and as far as he could imagine anybody seeing. Back in Illinois and Missouri the hills didn't reach so far but hedged in more. Out here everything seemed to be about twice as big, as though proportion had gotten out of hand and everything was twice as far or twice as broad, or twice as high, like the country had been made for men of double size. Bridger didn't have any words for how big it was or how empty it was, but he could feel the bigness and the emptiness inside.

When he lay in his robes that evening, he thought of the great sweep of plain around him, and this thicket the only place that was somehow sheltered, and they just one small spot against it all.

On the third morning Glass was still alive. Now he seemed delirious. He opened his eyes sometimes, although he didn't seem to see with them, and babbled things Bridger couldn't understand. He sat and waited, and listened to Fitzgerald muttering and cursing. It was amazing to him that Fitzgerald could have spent three days with him and not really spoken to him, just talked to himself or talked at Bridger. Some mountain men, Bridger noticed, got to be almost dumb brutes, after a while, that couldn't talk at all.

On the fourth morning Bridger wasn't sure for a while whether Glass was alive or dead. The chest didn't seem to move, and there were only the barest stirrings around the nose and mouth. He seemed to have gone into a sleep that was near to death. The fever was down some, though.

It was that afternoon that Fitzgerald finally talked to him. Suddenly friendly, he started hinting that he and Bridger were mighty good fellows to have stayed so long with Glass, risking their own necks. They had certainly gone more than forty dollars' worth. They had done it because they were not the kind that would walk off and leave a dying man and not try to help. But it would be terrible and not right if it turned out they'd have to stay a week or two weeks or goddamn knows how long until old Glass gave up. Nothing for it, of course, but it still wasn't right.

He kept on like that, gentle but clear, that day and evening. Glass stayed in the sleep that seemed near death. Perhaps he would just ease over to being dead any time now, without making a sign. The next morning he was the same. Fitzgerald kept angling back to how unfair it was, but gentle, because Bridger didn't take up his line. He knew where Fitzgerald was headed. That evening Glass was the same.

The next morning the stubborn old fellow opened his eyes. They were glazed, and at first Bridger wasn't sure whether he could see. Then he knew Glass could, and he told Fitzgerald.

'I'm glad he can see,' answered Fitzgerald, 'because he's going to need it.'

He started packing up. 'This niggur's getting out of here, Bridger. I think we've overstayed our time. Henry didn't mean for us to have to wait five days anyway, just for forty dollars. He thought we'd be right along. This ain't reasonable.' He was lashing his gear to their one horse. 'We used up our medicine, staying this long. This child ain't crazy.'

Bridger didn't say anything. He looked at Glass. His head was wagging back and forth. Might just be delirious. But Bridger thought he could see what was happening, and probably could hear, too. Bridger stared at him.

'I'm ready,' Fitzgerald said flatly. 'You coming or staying?'

'I can't go,' Bridger answered dully.

'Boy, I ain't gonna argue with you. It don't make no mind to me. But you know what they're gonna do to you, don't you? Maybe stick slivers of pine into you and light 'em, so you burn slow. Maybe skin you alive. This ain't no joke, boy, and no time for fancy notions.' Bridger said nothing. 'Get the hell off your ass and let's move. You ain't ready to throw it all away yet, not for a corpse.'

Bridger felt like his body was moving, not himself, like his legs were part of someone else and had their own orders. His whole body felt very, very heavy.

'Get his gear on there quick. I want to move.' Bridger looked at Fitzgerald, unbelieving. Fitzgerald barked, 'Get the gun and the knife and everything else put up here. You don't leave a dead man's things when you bury him. You take 'em along. And we buried old Glass. Remember that, boy.'

Bridger didn't look at Glass, but a glimpse out of the corner of one eye hinted that maybe Glass was trying to make a movement. He turned away. He walked alongside the horse in a stupor, and they were miles away before Bridger thought or felt anything again. Then he was violently angry, and maybe a little sick.

When Bridger and Fitzgerald left, Glass passed out. He didn't know how many days went by before he woke up. At first he wanted to holler and get them to come running back. But he knew it had been too long.

His body felt hot and he was aching for water. His tongue was dry and swollen, filling his mouth. He started to roll toward the spring, felt pain hit him like a club, and almost lost consciousness. He rested for a long time. Then he calculated slowly how he could do it. He rolled once, hard. The pain took his breath away. Then, lying on his stomach, he pivoted slowly until his face slid into wetness. He thought later that he might have slept a little before he drank. He noticed that the movements had gotten the bleeding started in thin trickles. He couldn't feel the gashes separately. His whole body pained him, and it must be pain that was keeping half his consciousness away. He slept.

He woke up alive, and thought that was a good start. He wanted food. Another good sign: dying men aren't hungry. A half-dozen buffalo berries hung low enough to reach, after he rolled onto his back. He would wait until tomorrow to try for more.

The next day Glass felt clearer in his head. First the berries: he had an idea. He would scoot to the base of the bush and put his weight on the branches, forcing them to the ground and breaking them so they would stay. Afterwards he felt like he had been trampled by a horse. He rested a long time before he scooted out to get the berries and spent the rest of the day in a kind of day-dream. He kept seeing Fitzgerald and Bridger leaving. He could go backwards some in his mind, and hear the words they said before they left—not all of them, and not clearly, but some of the words. Then he saw Bridger taking off his possibles and the two of them leave him empty-handed. When he woke up the next morning, Glass knew for the first time what had happened to him. He could put it in order in his mind. He spoke his first words, and they made him sure of it: 'Sons of bitches went off and left me to die. Took everything I had.' He spent the rest of the day mulling over that. Come morning, he had decided that he was going to get out of this hole, get up the river, and square accounts with Bridger and Fitzgerald. The ache to get square came on him like a new fever.

On the following day the desire for vengeance got a lucky break. Waking up from a nap, he saw a rattlesnake lazing nearby. It had just eaten a bird, and was swollen in the middle to the size of a man's fist. Hugh knew that he wouldn't even have to be especially agile. He slammed the rock down just in back of the rattler's head four or five times, cutting it in half. Then he shredded the meat, soaked the pieces in water, and fed himself like a baby. His medicine was good.

And when the sun came up one morning, just far enough to begin to warm things, he decided: he might as well move today as any day. He felt pretty good. He didn't know how many days had gone by since he met the grizzly, but enough of them. He might as well start for Fort Kiowa today.

Fort Kiowa it would have to be. That was a lot closer than Fort Henry. It was also generally downhill. And he could follow the river. A man who couldn't walk had best stay next to his water, and not set out across country towards the Yellowstone.

Because Hugh couldn't walk yet. He figured that if he waited till he could, his wait would outlast his food. Eating was his biggest worry. A lone man could make out in the Dakota, even if he was crawling, if he had a gun to shoot buffler and a knife to cut it with.

But those sons of bitches had taken both his knife and his rifle. Well, he would eat roots. Living with the Pawnees and knowing their ways came in handy sometimes.

Before that day was half over, he collapsed with weariness. He had begun by crawling along the creek. With every movement one of his wounds opened and bled. He nearly passed out a couple of times from the pain and was so weak that he felt like he was carrying a mule on his back. He had only been able to make about a mile all day, and he told himself that he would have to do better tomorrow because he didn't figure to get any stronger just eating roots. But telling himself didn't help. He wasn't sure that he could move at all tomorrow.

He did move, though. Another mile, and it felt about the same. On the third day he thought he went somewhat farther. But he would never make two hundred and fifty miles this way.

A couple of days later he heard wolves yipping close by on the plain. He crawled up the bank to take a look. They were harassing a buffalo calf. He watched with desperate hope while they brought the calf down and began to tear away the flesh ravenously. He waited and waited, calculating what he was going to do, until the calf was nearly half gone. He had to have that meat. But he had no hope of scaring off the wolves if he went up on all fours. They would see that he was a crippled man, and would attack, as a predator will attack any crippled enemy. He bided his time and got set in his mind.

At last the wolves slowed down in their gorging. They were full now, feeling heavy of belly and sluggish. Glass, taking along his driftwood club, crawled to within fifty yards of the carcass. Already the wolves had noticed him and were beginning to stir. He couldn't wait any longer. Leaning heavily on the club, he tried to stand up for the first time since Old Ephraim downed him. His mind reeled, and he felt like his body must be swaying like an old bull shot and about to fall. When he began to be steady, he held onto the club and cut loose with a fantastic screech, a Pawnee war cry. The wolves scattered a few feet and then began to ease back toward the calf. He walked straight forward now, depending on the club, letting loose with the screech again and again, rocking like a dinghy pitching on a heavy sea. The wolves slunk off.

When he reached the calf, Glass knelt down, clinging to his crutch, trying not to break his wounds open any worse. What blood he was losing, he thought, he would get back right here.

He tore at the raw flesh, and he stuffed great chunks into his mouth. I'm gonna live, he thought, I'm gonna live.

Hugh stayed by the carcass for several days, sleeping on the lee side at night, gorging himself on liver and heart and blood and intestine during the day. He stayed until the flesh began to go so bad that even he could smell it, used to it as he was.

When he left that spot, he was walking upright. It made him feel like a lord. Now he was high enough to see over the scrub bush that covered the plains. He could watch for bears, or Indians. He might be able to kill a rabbit or a badger if he was quick and lucky. But most of all it just felt different with his head up. Instead of staring into the sandy soil all the time, he could look around from horizon to horizon. He felt like a man again, not a four-legged crittur.

His wounds were better now. They all seemed to be on the way to healing, except for a bad one that was infected high on his back where he couldn't reach it. If he went slow and steady, he could make ten miles in a day now. He did go slow and steady. His mind bounced between jubilation at being alive to ornery vengefulness at having been left to die alone. The two drove him down the Grand to where it meets the Missouri and south along the great river towards Fort Kiowa. There Ashley was known and an Ashley man's credit would be good. He would get a new outfit, gun, knife, flint, powder, ball, and other possibilities. And from there he would turn around, head upriver, and get the men who abandoned him.

He made Fort Kiowa in the second week of October. It had been seven weeks since the grizzly had had her whacks at him. He had survived six of those weeks alone, and had risen from the state of near-corpse to crawl and walk some two hundred and fifty miles through hostile territory with no way to get meat and no protection from the marauding Rees. It astounded the trader Cayewa Brazeau, who ran Fort Kiowa.

Hugh was proud, but he was not enough impressed with himself to give his battered body a rest. Brazeau was outfitting a mackinaw to go up to the Mandan villages. The wilderness grapevine reported that the Rees had bought a village from the Mandans, who lived in permanent huts and not tipis. The Rees had given the peaceful Mandans a promise of good behaviour. Brazeau thought that now might be the time for a peaceful mission to re-establish trade with both tribes. He had six men, led by Antoine Citoleux and including the famous Charbonnau, of the Lewis and

Clark expedition, to make the journey. He was glad to add a seventh hand, Hugh Glass—though he must have thought the fellow was a bit queer, starting right out like that. After what Hugh had been through, though, it didn't seem like such a big deal. He'd made up his mind to the thing.

Citoleux was nervous. He made his will, just in case. The party began to get close to the Mandan villages, in what is now North Dakota, in the fourth week of November. Abruptly Charbonnau decided to get out and walk. The Ree village was a mile south of the Mandan village, and Tilton's Fort was up by the Mandans. Charbonnau wanted to circle around the Ree village on the west bank and go directly into Tilton's Fort. His medicine told him something. He trusted the Mandans, but not the Rees. The Frenchmen who made up the boat's crew just laughed. The next day Glass also put in to shore. The Missouri makes a considerable bend just below the villages. Hugh had no business at the villages or the fort. He could move faster and over a shorter route by himself cutting overland. So he set out.

A few miles across he saw several squaws. Rees, he noticed. They disappeared quickly. Glass figured they had gone for their men and started running. His wounds still bothered him some, and he couldn't make much time. Soon several braves came after him, mounted and screeching. Hugh saw he didn't have a chance. Maybe his luck, which had gotten him through two impossible situations, had just played out. Just when the Rees were within rifle shot, Glass heard hooves from the opposite direction. Mandans. Being ridden down from two sides, Hugh just stood and waited for whatever was going to happen. One of the Mandans pulled him up on the horse behind, and sprinted off towards the upper village.

The Rees had attracted the Mandans' attention with their whooping. The Mandans were tired of the Rees' troublemaking, and afraid that the whites might take their revenge against both tribes. So they delivered Hugh to their village, where he found Charbonnau. That evening, at the fort, they got the news that the party in the mackinaw had been slaughtered on the river by the Rees.

Hugh figured, with what he had come through, he didn't have much to worry about travelling on to Fort Henry. The next day he took off, only taking the precaution of walking along the east bank of the Missouri where he was less likely to run into Rees, Assiniboines, or Blackfeet. Most tribes were unpredictable; the

Blackfeet, alone among the plains tribes, were always hostile to whites. Had been, since John Colter had run away from them. Last time he heard, they had been plaguing Fort Henry like devils.

The snow was a foot deep now. Sometimes the wind swept down cuttingly from the north. The Missouri here flows through country bare of timber, and the wind could run unobstructed for miles. He hunted along the way, spent some cold nights, and got within sight of Fort Henry, 300 river miles from the Mandans, in less than three weeks. He tied some logs together with bark to cross the icy river. But he had already begun to suspect that something was wrong. In the fort he found only some friendly Sioux, exercising squatters' rights. The Henry brigade had gone up the Yellowstone, they said, to the Big Horn. That doubled the length of Hugh's lone journey, and took him still higher into mountain country. He started straight out through the snow.

On the night of December 31, 1823, Andrew Henry's brigade was celebrating the new year inside the new Fort Henry. They had reason: they had relocated from Blackfoot country to Crow country, after losing life after life to the Blackfeet. The Crows seemed nothing but friendly. The trapping in the fall hunt had equalled the Missouri trapping, if not topped it. They were finally about to take some beaver and make some money. They had found Indians who would trade pelts instead of stealing them. The country was good, sheltered enough, and with plenty of buffalo for the long winter. The life looked good.

They barely heard the pounding on the gate above the howling wind. Someone stumbled through the driving snow to open for whatever Indians might be there. What he saw he couldn't believe for a moment; the grizzled, hoar-frosted ghost of Hugh Glass, his hair, beard, and buckskins whitened by caked ice. Glass strode on into the room where the men were celebrating. The debauch stopped dead. 'It's Glass you're seeing,' Hugh said bluntly, 'where's Fitzgerald and Bridger?' One man edged forward and touched Hugh to see if he was solid. The others barraged him with questions he couldn't sort out, much less answer. 'It's Glass,' he said. 'Fitzgerald and Bridger went off and left me, goddamn 'em. Even took my rifle and my possibles. I been to Kiowa and the Mandans and I come to square with them. Where are they?'

Henry said that Fitzgerald was gone—gone downriver—given up and returned to the settlements. Why, Glass must have passed him on the river, him and Black Harris, going down in a canoe.

Henry stalled a bit. Harris was taking an express down to Ashley, he went on, and Fitzgerald and another fellow went with him—mustered out, just quit. Looks like Fitzgerald wasn't much account anyway.

'Don't back me off,' Glass snapped. 'Where in hell's Bridger?'

Stuck, Henry just pointed into a corner. Bridger had been shrinking there since Glass materialized from the dead. He had been shouldering a secret, festering wrong all these months, relieved only by the knowledge that dead men tell no tales. And here stood a dead man, sent back by the devils of hell against Jim Bridger, who more than half believed in ghosts. Stunned, he could hardly keep his mind conscious against the welling of guilt, hardly considering whether this spectre were dead or alive.

Hugh stared at the man he had pursued for a thousand miles. Bridger had the look of a man ready to be killed and go to hell for his mortal sin. He wasn't going to say anything. He looked pathetic, and pathetically young.

One of the two men he had pursued, Glass corrected himself. He remembered the scene of the two leaving him, and Bridger coming over and taking the rifle and knife. He hated Bridger. He remembered what he could of the words Fitzgerald had hit Bridger with at the time, words that struck fear into the boy. Glass wavered. Bridger had committed the unpardonable sin, not of God, but of the mountain men: never skip out on your friends in a fix. Glass glared at him. But he was just a boy.

'It's Glass, Bridger—the one you left to die, and not only left, but robbed. Robbed of them things as might have helped him survive, alone and crippled, on them plains. I came back because I swore I'd put you under. I had that notion in front of me when I crawled across the prairie starving and walked up the river alone, just to get this one job done, to make you a dead niggur like you tried to make me. But I see you're ashamed and sorry. I think you might have stayed by me if Fitzgerald hadn't got on you. You don't have to be afraid of me. I forgive you. You're just a kid.'

Bridger's face didn't show relief, or anything else in particular. He looked dazed or maybe sick. Glass felt lighter and easier, having gotten all those words out at once. He sat down, someone handed him a glass of whisky, and within a few minutes he had passed out.

Bridger felt almost nauseated with guilt and shame. He had been let off because he was a kid. He'd rather have been put under there and then.

When Glass woke up, he lazed around, thinking of starting downriver after Fitzgerald. The laze stretched on several days. The idea didn't seem to be goading him quite as hard now. He told himself that it was a bad winter, and he might as well wait for better weather. And he listened to himself.

In a few more days Glass found his vendetta route: Henry wanted to send a dispatch to Ashley. He intended to tell Ashley about the abandoning of the original Fort Henry, the new post among the Crows, and the upswing in business. And he wanted to add some bad news—that Ashley had better find another partner. Major Andrew Henry, who had been run out of the mountains by Blackfeet in 1810, had lost a lot of men and horses to the Blackfeet the last two years, and had had five casualties among thirteen men on last autumn's cross-country to the mouth of the Yellowstone, didn't care that business was looking good. Henry was the unluckiest brigade captain who ever led men into the mountains. He meant to quit the business, and fast—as soon as spring broke up the ice and he could get a boat down the Missouri.

Who better to take the message down to Ashley than Hugh Glass, who was demonstrably the luckiest man in the mountains and kept coming up when he should have gone down? As for Hugh, it meant he would be paid handsomely to make a trip he was going to make anyway, to get his revenge. The dispatch had to go to Fort Atkinson, where it could be taken by government courier to Ashley in St Louis. At the fort, Hugh would make inquiries about Fitzgerald, and track the bastard down. Four men, Marsh, Chapman, More, and Dutton, decided to go along to give the party some strength; two were going for company money, and two were quitting the mountains.

They left on February 29, 1824. Having in mind to miss the worst weather and take a shorter route besides, they went south, up the Powder River to its headwaters, and cross to the Platte River, instead of going northeast to the frozen Missouri and then southeast along the river; from there they could follow the river directly east to Fort Atkinson at Council Bluffs.

By the time they struck the Platte, spring was on its way and the ice was breaking up. Mountain men never walked where there was a river to carry them, so the five stopped and built a bullboat. The Platte was too shallow to float almost any kind of boat. Bullboats were the exception. They were generally saucer round, were made from buffalo skin stretched over limbs and caulked with buffalo fat, and had almost no draft. Glass and his comrades pushed off downstream close to the end of March. It looked like a lark to Hugh. He not only had companions, he was headed into the territory of his brothers, the Pawnees. Fat country to a mountain man, with plenty of buffalo, the sun warming the land with a gentle hand, the cottonwoods, beginning to turn green, and Indians who would treat him like a long-lost brother.

Where the Laramie comes into the Platte, where Fort Laramie was to be later on, the travellers spotted a sizable cluster of Indian lodges. Some braves came down the bank and waved, gave the sign language for peace, and called out for their white brothers to put in. Hugh would have paddled by, except for one thing the Indians couldn't guess: he recognized their lingo. They were Pawnees. He explained to his friends and put straight to the bank.

Hugh clambered out of the bullboat addressing the Indians in their own language, and identified himself as their brother and the son of one of their great chiefs. They put their arms around him, one at a time, and greeted him solemnly and gladly. He told the others to get out of the boat and come into the village. They were going to get a good feed. Besides, Pawnee women were as willing and as much fun as any squaws, and white men were still a novelty among them. And leave your rifles, he said. You don't need them, and it's an insult for a friend to bring weapons into a Pawnee camp. You might rile them.

Glass and three of his companions went to the tipi of the highest-ranking Indian and settled down for a smoke and a feed. Dutton stayed near the boat, suspicious. As the squaws were bustling around to serve their guests, Glass heard something telling: the language of the Pawnees and Rees was almost identical, but the Rees pronounced certain words differently. That squaw was a Ree. He knew by that way of talking. He looked around quickly and carefully. Impossible that the Rees could be three hundred miles from their territory. But he was sure now, and he spoke low: 'These are Rees. Let's cache.'

One of the leaders understood English and replied, 'No, we're Pawnees.' But Glass wasn't about to listen. The four cleared out and ran for the boat. The Rees came after them, screeching.

Dutton was already in mid-river in the bullboat when they reached the shore. Their rifles were gone, of course. They scattered.

Within five minutes Glass was crouched in a crevice in some rocks, hoping the Rees would miss him in the falling darkness. More was cut down in Glass's sight; then Chapman was killed close by. Glass huddled further down. While he waited for blackness, hearing nearby the awful cries of glee over the mutilated bodies, he figured out what had happened: the Rees had split up after the Arikara campaign. One band had gone to live with the Mandans; another band had disappeared westward, no one knew where. Well, they had come a long way to join their near-relatives the Pawnees, just where Glass would run into them. And they were mean as ever. Hell of a thing for a hoss to run in with the same band of Indians three times in nine months in three entirely different places and damn near get rubbed out three times. His luck was running bad.

Glass snuck out of the rocks and made some miles downriver before daylight. Then he cached in some rocks and took stock. Maybe his luck wasn't so bad after all. 'Although I had lost my rifle and all my plunder,' he said later, 'I felt quite rich when I found my knife, flint, and steel in my shot pouch. These little fixins make a man feel right peart when he is three or four hundred miles from anybody or any place.' Especially if the same man was left in the same fix eight months before without any fixins, and without able arms and legs. Wagh! He'd done it before and he could do it again. Besides, he still had Fitzgerald to even up with.

Hugh changed his aim from Fort Atkinson to Fort Kiowa. It was four hundred miles away, which was closer than Atkinson. He had no worry with food this time: the cows had recently dropped, and he could easily catch up with the calves only a few days old. He made meat as often as he felt inclined, and hit Fort Kiowa in May.

When he got on down to Fort Atkinson with the letter for Ashley, he got a couple of surprises and gave a couple. Dutton and Marsh had arrived before him, having joined up and come together down the Platte. They had reported him dead at last, and here he was again. The other surprise was mutual—with John Fitzgerald. Fitzgerald had heard that Glass was alive from Cayewa Brazeau up at Kiowa last December, and had been relieved to find out from Marsh and Dutton just a couple of weeks before that the old man had gone down. Yet here he was, not only alive, but murderous.

Hugh was right gratified to find Fitzgerald, until he found out one thing: Fitzgerald was now a member of the US Army, and killing him would get a man executed. Hugh blustered into the office of Captain Riley, demanding fair play. The officer brought Fitzgerald in.

Finally. There Fitzgerald stood, hangdog as Hugh could want. Funny, though, he couldn't hate the niggur quite as much as he wanted to. Maybe he'd had too much good luck of late to keep all that hating cached up inside. 'You ran out on me dyin',' he accused Fitzgerald. 'You was paid well enough, and you said you'd stay till I was good or gone down. But you got scared and run off. And you stole what I might have lived by. Stole it so you could get some money that wasn't yourn and so nobody'd know what you done. Well, I count you got something to think on the rest of your string.'

Riley dismissed Fitzgerald and made Glass an offer. If Glass would clear out, Riley would give him back his rifle and other possibles, and stake him what he needed to get started again. Hugh took it.

He decided, though, to try his luck somewhere else. He set out with a band headed for Santa Fe. For four years he trapped the streams of the Southwest. In 1829 he came back to Yellowstone country as a free trapper. In 1833 he tried his luck against the Rees once more. It had played out. Rees killed and scalped him and his companion, Edward Rose.

Glass, though, had become a grizzled legend to the men he shared robes, campfires, and fat cow with. He went jauntily at death four times in a row in one year, and came away with the upper hand. He had mountain luck. He showed incredible skill, endurance, and courage. With those, he survived in fact, and has survived in legend.

The Shaming of Broken Horn

Towards sundown of the second day after the train reached Fort Hall, Harlan Faber, elected wagon captain, called a meeting of the emigrant families, as was the custom when a question affecting them all had to be voted on. Well aware by now that this western land was a man's land in which a woman must keep silent, Mary Bailey told her pa she guessed she'd stay by their wagons and catch up on the mending. But her pa said, 'You got a right to be there. I want you to help me make up my mind which way to vote.'

'Your mind's already made up, isn't it, pa?'

'I know what I'd like to do, sure. But I want you at that meeting. Since your ma left us, you've taken her place, seems like.'

So Mary went along, carrying some mending with her to keep her hands busy, standing at the edge of the crowd with her lanky, grey-haired, slow-spoken pa, Jed, and her younger brother, Mike, who was slim, dark-eyed and, at fourteen, beginning to consider himself an adult. Mary, a pretty, black-haired, grave young lady of eighteen, had put away childish notions years ago.

Facing the crowd stood Harlan Faber. With him were Peter Kent, factor of Fort Hall; Broken Horn, the fierce-eyed Bannock chief whose imperious edict had brought on this present crisis; Tim Ramsey, guide for the wagon train; and a pair of American trappers who had drifted into the trading post the day before. Faber raised his hand for silence.

'You folks all know what this meeting's about. The trail forks here. What we got to decide is whether we want to go on to Oregon, like we'd planned, or change our plans and go to Californy.'

As the wagon captain outlined the situation facing the emigrants, Mary studied the two American trappers curiously, for there were strange tales of these wild, rootless men. Both wore ragged, grease-stained buckskins and had an alert, almost savage look about them. To the stooped, older man, Charley Huff, she gave no more than a brief glance; but the younger man, Dave Allen, standing so tall and straight, was so handsome and had such nice grey eyes that she stared at him shamelessly.

'If we go to Oregon,' Faber was saying, 'we'll have to pass through Bannock country. The Bannocks are on the warpath against Americans, Broken Horn says, an' will fight us every step of the way. But if we turn south an' head for Californy, stayin' clear of Bannock country, Broken Horn says his bucks won't pester us. That's how matters stand. Speak up, men, an' tell me how you feel.'

One by one the men spoke their sentiments, while their women-folk listened in silence. Jed whispered, 'Well, Mary?'

'It's up to you, pa. It's whatever you want to go.'

'It's the seedlings I'm thinkin' about. To bring a whole wagon-load of 'em this far, then give up—'

'Jed Bailey!' Faber called out. 'You got anything to say?'

New England born and bred, Jed shifted his weight from one foot to the other, cocked his head at the sky as if looking for sign of rain, then said slowly, 'Does it freeze in Californy, come winter?'

Tim Ramsey said no it didn't, normally. Peter Kent and the two trappers agreed. Faber let his eyes run over the crowd. 'Any more questions 'fore we take a vote?'

'Get on with it!' a man shouted. 'Call the roll!'

'All right.' Faber took a sheet of paper out of his pocket. 'Joshua Partridge.'

'Here!'

'I know you're here, you blamed fool! How do you vote?'

'Californy!'

'Frank Lutcher.'

'Californy!'

'Matthew Honleiker.'

'Californy!'

And so it went, down through the list until forty-nine names had been called. Now, with only one name left, the wagon captain paused, looked at Jed, then said, 'Jedidiah Bailey.'

Jed studied the blue sky and the far reach of parched land to the west. At last he said, 'A man can't grow decent apples in country where it don't freeze.'

'That ain't an answer, Jed. How do you vote?'

'Oregon.'

Mary heard a murmuring run through the crowd. 'Stubborn

old fool ... Jed Bailey and his damned apple trees ... Let him git scalped....'

Faber tallied the list. 'Results of the vote. Fer Californy, forty-nine. Fer Oregon, one. Majority rules, as agreed. We'll pull out first thing in the mornin' fer Californy.' He looked angrily at Jed. 'Forty-nine of us, anyhow. I wash my hands of you, Jed Bailey. Meetin's adjourned.'

The Bailey family walked back to their wagons in silence, Mary feeling proud of her pa, but not knowing how to put it into words. Mike went out to check on the grazing mules. Jed took a pair of wooden buckets and headed for the creek to get water for the seedlings. Mary readied supper. It being early July, dark came late and though the sun had sunk by the time she called her menfolk to supper—a good meat stew filled with fresh vegetables grown in the Fort Hall garden, baked beans sweetened with molasses, hot biscuits and dried-apple pie—there was still plenty of twilight left when they finished eating. Because she loved her pa and knew how worried he was, Mary treated him extra good.

'More pie, pa?'

'Thank you kindly, Mary, but I reckon not.' He gave her a gentle smile. 'You're a fine cook, girl, just like your ma was. The man that marries you will get a real prize.'

'Fiddlesticks!' Mary said, but the praise pleased her just the same.

Lighting his pipe, Jed brooded into the fire while Mike got out cleaning stick, rag and oil and set to work cleaning his rifle. Busy with the dishes, Mary did not hear the visitors approach until Peter Kent said, 'Good evening, Mr Bailey. May I have a word with you?'

'Sure. What's on your mind?'

Turning around, Mary got the fright of her life, for standing an arm's reach away was that murderous-looking Indian, Broken Horn. Likely she would have screamed if she hadn't looked past him and seen Charley Huff and Dave Allen. Dave Allen was smiling at her with those nice grey eyes, and somehow she knew nothing bad could happen when he was around. But watching Broken Horn sniff animal-like at the stew simmering in the iron pot and the pie keeping warm in the open Dutch oven, she did feel a mite uneasy.

'You're set on going to Oregon, I take it,' Kent said. 'Do you plan to wait here until an Oregon-bound train willing to fight its way through Bannock country comes along?'

'Can't hardly do that. Ours was the last train due to leave Independence this season.' A questioning look came into Jed's eyes. 'You got a proposition, Mr Kent?'

'Yes. Charley and Dave here also want to go to Oregon. I'll vouch for their reliability, if you want to hire them as guides. I've talked to Chief Broken Horn, and he's agreed—for a reasonable consideration—to let you pass through his country.'

'How much?'

'One hundred dollars.'

'And these gents, how much do they want?'

'Two hundred dollars—apiece.'

Jed fiddled with his pipe. 'That's a sight of money.'

'It's a sight of a job takin' two wagons an' three greenhorns through bad Injun country,' Charley grunted.

'There's one thing I must make clear,' Dave said, looking first at Mary, then at Jed. 'If you do hire us, you've got to do exactly as we tell you at all times.'

That was a mighty bossy way for a mere guide to talk, Mary thought angrily. Finishing the dishes, she carried them to the wagon and put them away. As she turned back to the fire, her mouth flew open in horror. Chief Broken Horn, fascinated by the smell emanating from the stewpot, had lifted its lid and was plunging a dirty butcher knife into its depths. This time she did scream.

'Stop that, you heathen!'

The Indian gave no sign that he heard her. Seizing the first weapon handy—a broom leaning against the wagon wheel—she made for him. As she raised the broom to strike, Dave Allen leaped toward her and caught her wrists.

'Easy, ma'am!'

Paying no attention to the commotion, Chief Broken Horn sniffed at the piece of meat he had impaled on his knife, diagnosed it as edible and disposed of it at a single bite. Finding the sample good, he dipped his bare hand into the pot, gobbled down its contents, then, still masticating noisily, stooped and picked up the apple pie. Indignantly Mary struggled against the steel-like grip on her wrists.

'Let me go!'

The nice grey eyes weren't smiling now. 'Don't you want to go to Oregon?'

'Of course I do!'

'You won't get there by beating Indian chiefs on the head with a broom. If you hit Broken Horn, he'd be so insulted he'd kill us all first chance he got!'

It was too late to save the pie anyway, so Mary let go of the broom. 'All right, Mr Allen. I won't harm your precious Indian. Now let me go.'

The grin came back to his face, and he released her. 'That's better.' He turned to Jed. 'Think you can control your daughter?'

Jed looked questioningly at Mary. Shamefaced, she dropped her gaze to the ground. She was still trembling with anger, not only at Chief Broken Horn but also at these two trappers who, to her way of thinking, were heartlessly taking advantage of her pa. Why, five hundred dollars was half of the family's lifetime savings! But this was a man's world, and it was not her place to object.

'I'll make no trouble, pa. I promise.'

'That's sensible talk,' Dave said. He nodded to Jed. 'It's set, then. We'll pull out first thing in the morning.'

West of Fort Hall the trail followed Snake River across flat, monotonous sagebrush desert, with mountains faint in the heat-hazed distance to the northwest and the green, swift-flowing river often lost deep in lava-walled canyons. Jed drove one wagon, Mary the other, except when the road got too bad, at which times Dave would tie his saddle horse to the tail gate, climb to the driver's seat and take the reins. He drove as he did everything else, with a casual skill which the mules recognized and responded to, though the stubborn brutes gave Mary all kinds of trouble.

'Good mules,' he said, grinning at her as the wagon topped a particularly bad grade. 'How come Jed was smart enough to use mules instead of oxen?'

'Pa is a smart man.'

'What's he going to do with those seedlings?'

'Raise apples. Back home he had the finest apple orchard in the state.'

'Why did you leave?'

'Ma died a year ago, and it took the heart out of pa. He got restless, hearing about the free land in Oregon and how scarce fresh fruit was out there. He kept talking about it, and I thought a change might do him good.'

The wagon was on a perfectly level stretch of trail now, and there was no reason why Dave shouldn't turn the reins over to her, but he lingered. 'Kind of hard on a woman, ain't it, leaving her friends and all?'

'Pa and Mike are all that matter to me.'

'Most girls of your age think more of catching a husband than they do of their pa and brother.'

The way he put it exasperated her. 'You make getting married sound like trapping.'

He threw back his head and laughed heartily. 'I meant no offence. But judging from what I've seen of women, most of 'em do have men on their minds when they get to be your age.'

'I'll bet they pestered you no end when you lived in civilized country.'

'Well, they did, if you want the truth.'

'Is that why you ran away and turned trapper?'

'Nope. I just wanted to see what was on the other side of the hill.'

'Did you find out?'

'Sure. Another hill—with another side to it.' He stopped the wagon, handed her the reins and climbed down. Mounting his horse, he said with a grin, 'Don't say anything to those mules, gal. Maybe they'll think I'm still driving and won't give you no trouble.'

Angrily she watched him gallop away. Then she gave the off-wheeler a lick with the whip that made him jump as if he'd been scalded.

For a week they travelled west without molestation, save for the torment of heat, dust and monotony. Dave said the fact that they saw no Indians didn't mean the Indians hadn't seen them. Chief Broken Horn had ridden ahead, he said, to warn his people that the party of whites was coming; and scouts watching from ridge tops likely were noting the progress of the wagons.

'We won't be safe,' Dave said, ''till we're into the Blue Mountains. And we'll have company before we get out of Bannock country, you can bet on that. When we do, Charley and I will tell you how to behave. Make sure you listen.'

The two trappers had brought along several extra horses to pack their gear, and when Charley suggested that one of the animals' loads be stowed in a wagon, freeing the horse for Mike to ride and accompany him on hunts for fresh meat, the old trapper made himself a friend for life.

From dawn till dusk, Mike tagged after Charley, listening with youthful awe to Charley's rambling tales of beaver trapping, Indian fighting and wilderness adventures. Mary was aware of the relationship that existed between boy and man, but she saw no harm in it.

One evening they camped in a grassy swale bare of trees, with the river five hundred feet below. It was quite a chore lugging up water for the seedlings; and by the time it was finished, Jed was done in. He lay down on the ground with a weary sigh.

'Jehoshaphat, I'm tired! Hungry too. What's for supper, Mary?'

Mary was exhausted; the fuel was scant, and what there was of it refused to burn. 'Nothing,' she said shortly, 'unless somebody fetches me some decent firewood.'

'Mike,' Jed said, 'cut your sister some wood. Hustle, now!'

Charley and Mike were squatting nearby, the old trapper rambling on while the boy listened intently. Mary gave her brother a sharp look. 'Mike!'

'Hmm?'

'Did you hear your pa?'

'What'd he say?'

'He told you to fetch me some firewood.'

'Aw, fetch it yourself. That's squaw work.'

Mary stared at her brother. Jed sat up with a scowl. 'What did you say, son?'

Mike flushed, gave Charley a sidelong glance and muttered, 'Cutting firewood is squaw work. Ain't it, Charley?'

'Why, yeah, boy,' Charley answered, scratching his ribs. 'Amongst Injuns, that's how it is. The buck kills the game an' brings it home, an' his squaw skins an' cooks it.'

Dave, who had just strolled up, looked at Mike and said, 'Don't believe everything Charley tells you, son.'

'But Charley knows all about squaws!' Mike said indignantly. 'He's had dozens of 'em! ... Haven't you, Charley?'

'Wal, not dozens—'

Mary put her hands on her hips. 'I never heard the like! Stuffing a boy full of awful stories!'

'Mike, fetch Mary some wood,' Dave said firmly. 'Jump, now! ... Charley, you help him.'

Charley looked hurt. 'Me? Me fetch wood?'

'If you want to eat, you'd better.'

After supper, Mary strolled off into the twilight and sat down on a boulder overlooking the whispering river. Though she'd promised her pa she'd make no trouble, the chore of feeding four hungry, ungrateful men three times a day was getting on her nerves; and she knew if she had to listen to any more of their idle chatter, she'd likely bust loose and say something she'd regret. Hearing a quiet step behind her, she looked around. Dave had followed her.

'Nice night.'

'Yes.'

'You'd ought not to wander away from camp alone. Some Injun might see you and pack you home with him.'

'Just let one try.'

Sitting down beside her, he lit his pipe. 'Charley don't mean no harm. He just likes to tell big windies.'

'Has he had many squaws?'

'Two or three.'

'Did he—marry them?'

'Bought 'em.'

She stared at him, not sure whether he was teasing her or telling the blunt truth. Deciding he was telling the truth, she exclaimed, 'Do you mean to say Indian women are bought and sold like—like horses?'

'Sure. A man picks out a squaw he wants, dickers with her pa and settles on a price. Some come higher than others, naturally. You take a young, healthy woman that's a good cook, she'll cost a man a sight more than a run-of-the-mill squaw would.'

'What if she doesn't like the man that buys her? What if she refuses to live with him?'

'Why, he beats her. That generally makes her behave.'

'I think that's horrible!'

His eyes were twinkling, and now the suspicion came to her that he hadn't been telling the truth. She was dying to ask him if he'd ever owned any squaws, but blessed if she'd give him a chance to tease her further. Grinning, he held out his hand and helped her up. 'Come on, you'd better get back to camp. You're too good a cook to lose.'

The Bannocks appeared while they were nooning next day. Seeing the squaws and children in the band, Dave said their intentions likely were peaceable, for Indians didn't take their families along when they had war in mind. But watching the savages set up their tepees a quarter of a mile down the valley, Mary felt uneasy.

Chief Broken Horn, accompanied by half a dozen of the leaders of the tribe, rode into camp presently. Broken Horn made a long speech, emphasized by many dramatic gestures. The gist of it was, Dave said, that Broken Horn considered himself quite a great man.

Had he not made forty-nine wagons turn aside from the Oregon trail because the American emigrants feared him? Was it not only through his generosity and by his consent that this small party was being permitted to cross his lands after paying the toll he demanded?

'Can't say as I like that kind of talk,' Jed muttered.

'Let him brag,' Dave said. 'It don't hurt us a bit.'

When the chief finished his speech, Dave frowned, then came over to Mary and said, 'We're going to have company for supper.'

'Chief Broken Horn?'

'Yeah. He and six of his headmen. You're to fix them a big feed, he says, with lots of stew and pie like you cooked for him back at Fort Hall.'

'I didn't cook anything for him! He stole that food, and you know it.'

'Well, he tells it different. Anyhow he seems to like your cooking and wants more of it.'

'Do you mean to tell me I've got to feed seven of those heathens?'

'Afraid so. He says when he eats well, his dreams are good. He says if his dreams are good tonight, he'll let us go on in peace. But if his dreams are bad—'

'Now, look here!' Jed cut in angrily. 'The old thief made a bargain and he's got to stick to it, good dreams or bad!'

'We've got to humour him,' Dave said, shaking his head. He looked at Mary. 'Can you do it? Can you rustle up enough stew and pie to make them happy?'

Mary was tired and she was scared, but most of all, right now, she was mad. Seemed like all she'd done since she'd left home was cater to men, cooking for them, washing for them, mending for them. She hadn't minded doing those chores for her own family because that was her job. But if this was a man's land, why didn't the men out here act like men? Why had Harlan Faber and the other men back at Fort Hall let an arrogant old Indian turn them aside from their original destination? Why didn't Charley and Dave make Chief Broken Horn live up to his promise with no nonsense about dreams?

'All right,' she said wearily. 'I'll feed them. But you'll all have to help me.'

Charley and Mike had killed an antelope and two deer the evening before, so meat was no problem. There was still half a barrel of dried apples left in the wagon, plenty of beans, sugar and flour, fifty pounds of potatoes she'd bought at Fort Hall, and a few carefully hoarded onions, carrots and dried peas. While Charley chopped wood and Dave carried water, she had Mike stretch a large square of canvas on the ground beside one of the wagons—on this her guests would sit. Brushing aside her pa's objections that it was casting pearls before swine, she made him dig out the family's best china, silverware, glasses, pitcher and a white linen tablecloth, which she laid and set on the canvas ground cloth. Except for the fact that her banquet table had no legs, it looked as attractive as any she'd ever set back home.

How much food could a hungry Indian eat? She made a liberal estimate of what a normal man with a healthy appetite could do away with at one sitting and tripled it, just to be on the safe side. She took special care that there should be more apple pie than her guests could possibly consume.

After putting a quantity of dried apples to soak for several hours, she prepared two dozen pie shells. When the apples had soaked sufficiently, she filled the shells, covered them with thin strips of dough, coated them with brown sugar and baked them until they were almost done. One of her most precious culinary treasures was a square tin of grated cheese flakes, which time and the dry western air had long since drawn all moisture from, but which, when sprinkled generously over the top of an apple pie and heated for a few minutes, melted and blended with the sugar to give the pie a delightful flavour. The tin was kept in a wooden chest in the wagon, along with her spices, extracts and family medical supplies. She asked Mike to get it for her.

Climbing into the wagon, he rummaged around, then called, 'Is it the red tin?'

'No, the blue one. Hurry, Mike!'

He clambered out of the wagon and handed her the tin. Taking a tablespoon, she hurriedly ladled a liberal layer of powdery flakes over the top of each pie, set them back in the Dutch ovens to bake and turned her attention to other tasks. Some minutes later she was exasperated to find Mike, whom she had told to return the tin to the chest, curiously staring down at what remained of its contents.

'Mike, will you please quit dawdling and put that away?'

'How come you sprinkled this stuff on the pies?'

'Because it's cheese, you idiot!'

'Don't smell like cheese,' He dipped finger and thumb into the tin, took a tiny pinch, sampled it. 'Don't taste like cheese either.'

She stared at the tin in horror. It wasn't blue. It was green.

And pasted on its side was a faded label. She read it and suddenly felt faint. 'Oh, my goodness!'

She ran to one of the Dutch ovens, opened it and snatched out a pie. Heedless of scorched fingers, she tried a tiny sample of the browned, delicious-looking crust. Mike did the same. He made a face.

'You going to feed these pies to the Indians?'

She closed her eyes and tried to think. The stuff wouldn't kill them, of that she was sure. It was too late to bake more pies, certainly, for even now the guests were arriving. Dressed in their finest, followed at a respectful distance by a horde of curious squaws, children and uninvited braves, Chief Broken Horn and his subchiefs had dismounted from their horses and were walking into camp. Worn-out and nerve-ragged after her long afternoon of work, Mary felt like dropping to the ground and giving way to tears. Instead she got mad. She got so mad that she didn't care a hang what happened, just so long as those pies didn't go to waste. Opening her eyes, she gave her brother a grim look.

'I certainly am. Get me the sugar, Mike. Indians will eat anything if it's sweet enough.'

Judging from the amount of food consumed and the rapidity with which it vanished, the feast was a huge success. The Indians were vastly fascinated by the plates, dishes and silverware, though they used their bare hands more than they did the knives, forks and spoons. The cold tea, liberally sugared, was a great hit, too, disappearing as fast as Mike could fill the glasses. And the pie brought forth approving grunts from all.

Mary had given her own menfolk strict orders not to partake of the pie, telling them that she feared there might not be enough to go round; but as the Indians one by one lapsed into glassy-eyed satiety, with half a dozen still uneaten pies before them, Dave gazed longingly at the beautiful creation on the tablecloth between himself and Chief Broken Horn. He smiled up at Mary.

'Sure does look like fine pie. Can't I have a piece?'

'No,' Mary said sharply.

'Not even a little one?' he persisted, picking up the pie. 'Why, if you knew how long it's been since I tasted—'

'I said "no",' Mary cut in, rudely snatching the pie out of his hand. Pretending that she'd done it for the sake of her guests, she turned to Chief Broken Horn and smiled. 'More pie, Mr Broken Horn?'

The Indian made a sign indicating he was full up to his chin.

As he looked her over from head to toe, a greedy acquisitive light came into his black eyes. He turned and grunted something to Dave. Dave laughed and winked at Mary.

'He says you're a better cook than his own squaw is.'

'That's very kind of him.'

'He wants to know if your pa will sell you. He says he'd pay a fancy price.'

Mary was too tired to have much of a sense of humour right then. From the way Jed's face froze, he wasn't in a joking mood either. 'I won't stand for that kind of talk in front of Mary.'

'He didn't mean it as an insult,' Dave said. 'He meant it as a—'

Chief Broken Horn showed exactly how he had meant it by reaching up, seizing Mary's left wrist and pulling her toward him. Livid-faced, Jed leaped to his feet. Dave swore and reached for the pistol in his belt. Charley drew his knife. Mike ran and grabbed up his rifle. But Mary was too angry to wait for help from her menfolk. Quick as a wink, she drew back her right arm and plastered Chief Broken Horn full in the face with the apple pie.

For a moment there wasn't a sound. The Indians were all staring at their chief, who lay flat on his back—pawing pie out of his eyes, kicking his heels in the air in a most unchieftain-like manner.

Getting his feet under him, Chief Broken Horn gave Mary a stunned, horrified glance, then wheeled and ran for his horse as if all the hounds of hell were after him. The other Indians wasted no time in following.

Mary took a long, deep breath. Turning to look at Jed, she said in a voice filled with shame, 'I'm sorry, pa.'

'Don't be,' Dave said, and his nice grey eyes were hard as flint. 'If you hadn't done what you did, I'd have killed him where he sat.'

A body does queer things in time of stress. Suddenly becoming aware of the way her menfolk were staring at her, their weapons in their hands, their eyes filled with amazement, relief and admiration, she began to laugh. She laughed till tears ran out of her eyes, but for the life of her she couldn't stop. Dave put an arm around her shoulders and said gently, 'Easy, Mary—easy.'

She sighed and quietly fainted.

As dark came on and the fires burned low, they sat huddled together, their backs against a wagon for safety's sake, listening to the drums in the Indian village. Mary was frightened now, but looking around, seeing the grim looks on the faces of her menfolk as they balanced their rifles across their knees, she was sure of one thing—her men would act like men if the need arose, and she was proud of them all.

'What do you think they'll do?' Jed said.

'Hard to tell,' Dave answered. 'Broken Horn has lost considerable face, being made a fool of by a woman in public. If there's going to be an attack, it will likely come at dawn. He'll spend the night stirring up the young bucks. The war drums are going already.'

Charley, who had been listening intently to the sounds coming from the village, interrupted, 'Quiet, boy!'

'What's the matter?'

'Them drums. They don't sound like war drums to me. Sound more like medicine drums.'

'What's the difference?' Mary asked.

Patiently Dave explained that when Bannocks prepared for battle, the drums were pounded in one fashion; but when there was sickness in the tribe and the medicine man was called in to recite his chants and attempt to heal the ill person, the drums were beaten in another manner. 'But Charley's wrong,' he added. 'Chief Broken Horn isn't going to let his medicine man fool around curing sick people tonight.'

'Maybe he's sick. Eating all that food—'

'He's got the stomach of a wolf. No, they're war drums, no question about that,' Dave insisted.

In the faint glow of the dying fires Mary saw a bulky figure appear on the far side of camp. Dave called out a challenge in the Bannock tongue and was quickly answered by an Indian woman. He told her to approach the wagon, and she did so—her hesitant pace showing how frightened she was. She was fat, wrinkled and middle-aged. Dave asked her who she was and what she wanted. As she spoke, he translated.

'She says she's Broken Horn's squaw.'

'Is he going to attack?' Jed said.

'She says no.'

'So he's going to stick to his bargain after all?'

'But the young bucks might, she says, if they can work up nerve enough. They're arguing it out now.'

'Can't he keep them in line?'

Mary saw Dave frown as the squaw spoke. 'She says he ain't interested in anything right now except the mess of bad spirits that have crawled into his belly. She says he's sick as a dog—and so are all the other chiefs that ate with us.' Dave turned and gave Mary a sharp look. 'She thinks you poisoned 'em.'

'I didn't!'

'How come they all took sick, then?'

Mary flushed. 'Maybe it was the beans and all that cold tea they drank.'

'It was the apple pie, wasn't it? You wouldn't let us eat any of it, but you made sure they stuffed themselves with it. What did you put in that pie, Mary?'

Defiantly Mary looked at Dave. 'Epsom salts.'

'What?'

'It won't hurt them. In fact, they made such pigs of themselves, it might even do them some good. Why, I wouldn't be surprised but what they all dream real nice dreams—when they finally get to sleep. That's what you wanted, wasn't it?'

Dave looked shaken. In fact, all her menfolk were staring at her, awe and respect in their eyes. Suddenly the squaw started gabbling furiously, pointing an accusing finger at Mary. Dave listened for a time, then he silenced her with a gesture.

'She says either you poisoned her man or cast an evil spell on him because he grabbed hold of you. Whichever it was you did, she's begging you to make him well. What shall I tell her?'

Mary smiled. 'Tell her I cast a spell.'

'Now, look here!'

'Tell her, please. Tell her that all white women have the power to cast spells over men when they get angry with them.'

Reluctantly Dave spoke to the Indian woman. Her black eyes grew wide with fright as she stared at Mary, then she grunted a question. Dave said, 'She wants to know how long the spell will last.'

'Tell her two days. Tell her if her husband and the other sick chiefs lie quietly for two days and nights, thinking nothing but peaceful thoughts, they will get well. But if they let their people attack us, they will die.'

An admiring grin spread over Dave's face. 'Now why didn't I think of that?'

As he spoke to the squaw, Mary saw the frightened look fade from the woman's face. The squaw nodded vigorously, turned to go, hesitated; then shyly walked up to Mary, touched Mary's breast, then her own, grunted something and ran off into the darkness. Mary looked at Dave.

'What did that mean?'

Dave didn't answer for a moment. Then, an uneasy light coming into his nice grey eyes, as if he were looking into the future, he answered, 'She says you know how to handle men and she's glad you hit her husband with that pie. She's been wanting to sock the old fool for years.'

Donald Hamilton

The Guns of William Longley

We'd been up north delivering a herd for Old Man Butcher the summer I'm telling about. I was nineteen at the time. I was young and big, and I was plenty tough, or thought I was, which amounts to the same thing up to a point. Maybe I was making up for all the years of being that nice Anderson boy, back in Willow Fork, Texas. When your dad wears a badge, you're kind of obliged to behave yourself around home so as not to shame him. But Pop was dead now, and this wasn't Texas.

Anyway, I was tough enough that we had to leave Dodge City in something of a hurry after I got into an argument with a fellow who, it turned out, wasn't nearly as handy with a gun as he claimed to be. I'd never killed a man before. It made me feel kind of funny for a couple of days, but like I say, I was young and tough then, and I'd seen men I really cared for trampled in stampedes and drowned in rivers on the way north. I wasn't going to grieve long over one belligerent stranger.

It was on the long trail home that I first saw the guns one evening by the fire. We had a blanket spread on the ground, and we were playing cards for what was left of our pay—what we hadn't already spent on girls and liquor and general hell-raising. My luck was in, and one by one the others dropped out, all but Waco Smith, who got stubborn and went over to his bedroll and hauled out the guns.

'I got them in Dodge,' he said. 'Pretty, ain't they? Fellow I bought them from claimed they belonged to Bill Longley.'

'Is that a fact?' I said, like I wasn't much impressed. 'Who's Longley?'

I knew who Bill Longley was, all right, but a man's got a right to dicker a bit, and besides, I couldn't help devilling Waco now and then. I liked him all right, but he was one of those cocky little fellows who ask for it. You know the kind. They always know everything.

I sat there while he told me about Bill Longley, the giant from Texas with thirty-two killings to his credit, the man who was hanged twice. A bunch of vigilantes strung him up once for horse-stealing he hadn't done, but the rope broke after they'd ridden off and he dropped to the ground, kind of short of breath but alive and kicking.

Then he was tried and hanged for a murder he had done, some years later in Giddings, Texas. He was so big that the rope gave way again and he landed on his feet under the trap, making six-inch-deep footprints in the hard ground—they're still there in Giddings to be seen, Waco said, Bill Longley's footprints—but it broke his neck this time and they buried him nearby. At least a funeral service was held, but some say there's just an empty coffin in the grave.

I said, 'This Longley gent can't have been so much, to let folks keep stringing him up that way.'

That set Waco off again, while I toyed with the guns. They were pretty, all right, in a big carved belt with two carved holsters, but I wasn't much interested in leatherwork. It was the weapons themselves that took my fancy. They'd been used but someone had looked after them well. They were handsome pieces, smooth-working, and they had a good feel to them. You know how it is when a firearm feels just right. A fellow with hands the size of mine doesn't often find guns to fit him like that.

'How much do you figure they're worth?' I asked, when Waco stopped for breath.

'Well, now,' he said, getting a sharp look on his face, and I came home to Willow Fork with the Longley guns strapped around me. If that's what they were.

I got a room and cleaned up at the hotel. I didn't much feel like riding clear out to the ranch and seeing what it looked like with Ma and Pa gone two years and nobody looking after things. Well, I'd put the place on its feet again one of these days, as soon as I'd had a little fun and saved a little money. I'd buckle right down to it, I told myself, as soon as Junellen set the date, which I'd been after her to do since before my folks died. She couldn't keep saying forever we were too young.

I got into my good clothes and went to see her. I won't say she'd been on my mind all the way up the trail and back again, because it wouldn't be true. A lot of the time I'd been too busy or tired for dreaming, and in Dodge City I'd done my best *not* to think of her, if you know what I mean. It did seem like a young fellow engaged to a beautiful girl like Junellen Barr could have behaved himself better up there, but it had been a long dusty drive and you know how it is.

But now I was home and it seemed like I'd been missing Junellen every minute since I left, and I couldn't wait to see her. I walked along the street in the hot sunshine feeling light and happy. Maybe my leaving my guns at the hotel had something to do with the light feeling, but the happiness was all for Junellen, and I ran up the steps to the house and knocked on the door. She'd have heard we were back and she'd be waiting to greet me, I was sure.

I knocked again and the door opened and I stepped forward eagerly. 'Junellen—' I said, and stopped foolishly.

'Come in, Jim,' said her father, a little turkey of a man who owned the drygoods store in town. He went on smoothly: 'I understand you had quite an eventful journey. We are waiting to hear all about it.'

He was being sarcastic, but that was his way, and I couldn't be bothered with trying to figure what he was driving at. I'd already stepped into the room, and there was Junellen with her mother standing close as if to protect her, which seemed kind of funny. There was a man in the room, too, Mr Carmichael from the bank, who'd fought with Pa in the war. He was tall and handsome as always, a little heavy nowadays but still dressed like a fashion plate. I couldn't figure what he was doing there.

It wasn't going at all the way I'd hoped, my reunion with Junellen, and I stopped, looking at her.

'So you're back, Jim,' she said. 'I heard you had a real exciting time. Dodge City must be quite a place.'

There was a funny hard note in her voice. She held herself very straight, standing there by her mother, in a blue-flowered dress that matched her eyes. She was a real little lady, Junellen. She made kind of a point of it, in fact, and Martha Butcher, old Man Butcher's kid, used to say about Junellen Barr that butter wouldn't melt in her mouth, but that always seemed like a silly saying to me, and who was Martha Butcher anyway, just because her daddy owned a lot of cows?

Martha'd also remarked about girls who had to drive two front names in harness as if one wasn't good enough, and I'd told her it surely wasn't if it was a name like Martha, and she'd kicked me on the the shin. But that was a long time ago when we were all kids.

Junellen's mother broke the silence, in her nervous way: 'Dear, hadn't you better tell Jim the news?' She turned to Mr Carmichael. 'Howard, perhaps you should—'

Mr Carmichael came forward and took Junellen's hand. 'Miss Barr has done me the honour to promise to be my wife,' he said.

I said, 'But she can't. She's engaged to me.'

Junellen's mother said quickly, 'It was just a childish thing, not to be taken seriously.'

I said, 'Well, I took it seriously!'

Junellen looked up at me. 'Did you, Jim? In Dodge City, did you?' I didn't say anything. She said breathlessly, 'It doesn't matter. I suppose I could forgive.... But you have killed a man. I could never love a man who has taken a human life.'

Anyway, she said something like that. I had a funny feeling in my stomach and a roaring sound in my ears. They talk about your heart breaking, but that's where it hit me, the stomach and the ears. So I can't tell you exactly what she said, but it was something like that.

I heard myself say, 'Mr Carmichael spent the war peppering Yanks with a pea-shooter, I take it.'

'That's different—'

Mr Carmichael spoke quickly. 'What Miss Barr means is that there's a difference between a battle and a drunken brawl, Jim. I am glad your father did not live to see his son wearing two big guns and shooting men down in the street. He was a fine man and a good sheriff for this county. It was only for his memory's sake that I agreed to let Miss Barr break the news to you in person. From what we hear of your exploits up north, you have certainly forfeited all right to consideration from her.'

There was something in what he said, but I couldn't see that it was his place to say it. 'You agreed?' I said. 'That was mighty kind of you, sir, I'm sure.' I looked away from him. 'Junellen—'

Mr Carmichael interrupted. 'I do not wish my fiancée to be distressed by a continuation of this painful scene. I must ask you to leave, Jim.'

I ignored him. 'Junellen,' I said, 'is this what you really—'

Mr Carmichael took me by the arm. I turned my head to look at him again. I looked at the hand with which he was holding me. I waited. He didn't let go. I hit him and he went back across the room and kind of fell into a chair. The chair broke under him. Junellen's father ran over to help him up. Mr Carmichael's mouth was bloody. He wiped it with a handkerchief.

I said, 'You shouldn't have put your hand on me, sir.'

'Note the pride,' Mr Carmichael said, dabbing at his cut lip. 'Note the vicious, twisted pride. They all have it, all these young toughs. You are too big for me to box, Jim, and it is an undignified thing anyway. I have worn a sidearm in my time. I will go to the bank and get it, while you arm yourself.'

'I will meet you in front of the hotel, sir,' I said, 'if that is agreeable to you.'

'It is agreeable,' he said, and went out.

I followed him without looking back. I think Junellen was crying, and I know her parents were saying one thing and another in high, indignant voices, but the funny roaring was in my ears and I didn't pay too much attention. The sun was very bright outside. As I started for the hotel, somebody ran up to me.

'Here you are, Jim.' It was Waco, holding out the Longley guns in their carved holsters. 'I heard what happened. Don't take any chances with the old fool.'

I looked down at him and asked, 'How did Junellen and her folks learn about what happened in Dodge?'

He said, 'It's a small town, Jim, and all the boys have been drinking and talking, glad to get home.'

'Sure,' I said, buckling on the guns. 'Sure.'

It didn't matter. It would have got around sooner or later, and I wouldn't have lied about it if asked. We walked slowly towards the hotel.

'Dutch LeBaron is hiding out back in the hills with a dozen men,' Waco said. 'I heard it from a man in a bar.'

'Who's Dutch LeBaron?' I asked. I didn't care, but it was something to talk about as we walked.

'Dutch?' Waco said. 'Why, Dutch is wanted in five states and a couple of territories. Hell, the price on his head is so high now even Fenn is after him.'

'Fenn?' I said. He sure knew a lot of names. 'Who's Fenn?'

'You've heard of Old Joe Fenn, the bounty hunter. Well, if he comes after Dutch, he's asking for it. Dutch can take care of himself.'

'Is that a fact?' I said, and then I saw Mr Carmichael coming, but he was a way off yet and I said, 'You sound like this Dutch fellow was a friend of yours—'

But Waco wasn't there anymore. I had the street to myself, except for Mr Carmichael, who had a gun strapped on outside his fine coat. It was an army gun in a black army holster with a flap, worn cavalry style on the right side, butt forward. They wear them like that to make room for the sabre on the left, but it makes a clumsy rig.

I walked forward to meet Mr Carmichael, and I knew I would have to let him shoot once. He was a popular man and a rich man and he would have to draw first and shoot first or I would be in serious trouble. I figured it all out very coldly, as if I had been killing men all my life. We stopped, and Mr Carmichael undid the flap of the army holster and pulled out the big cavalry pistol awkwardly and fired and missed, as I had known, somehow, that he would.

Then I drew the right-hand gun, and as I did so I realized that I didn't particularly want to kill Mr Carmichael. I mean, he was a brave man coming here with his old cap-and-ball pistol, knowing all the time that I could outdraw and outshoot him with my eyes closed. But I didn't want to be killed, either, and he had the piece cocked and was about to fire again. I tried to aim for a place that wouldn't kill him, or cripple him too badly, and the gun wouldn't do it.

I mean, it was a frightening thing. It was like I was fighting the Longley gun for Mr Carmichael's life. The old army revolver fired once more and something rapped my left arm lightly. The Longley gun went off at last, and Mr Carmichael spun around and fell on his face in the street. There was a cry, and Junellen came running and went to her knees beside him.

'You murderer!' she screamed at me. 'You hateful murderer!'

It showed how she felt about him, that she would kneel in the dust like that in her blue-flowered dress. Junellen was always very careful of her pretty clothes. I punched out the empty and replaced it. Dr Sims came up and examined Mr Carmichael and said he was shot in the leg, which I already knew, being the one who had shot him there. Dr Sims said he was going to be all right, God willing.

Having heard this, I went over to another part of town and tried to get drunk. I didn't have much luck at it, so I went into the place next to the hotel for a cup of coffee. There wasn't anybody in the place but a skinny girl with an apron on.

I said, 'I'd like a cup of coffee, ma'am,' and sat down.

She said, coming over, 'Jim Anderson, you're drunk. At least you smell like it.'

I looked up and saw that it was Martha Butcher. She set a cup down in front of me. I asked, 'What are you doing here waiting tables?'

She said, 'I had a fight with Dad about ... well, never mind what it was about. Anyway, I told him I was old enough to run my own life and if he didn't stop trying to boss me around like I was one of the hands, I'd pack up and leave. And he laughed and asked what I'd do for money, away from home, and I said I'd earn it, so here I am.'

It was just like Martha Butcher, and I saw no reason to make a fuss over it like she probably wanted me to.

'Seems like you are,' I agreed. 'Do I get sugar, too, or does that cost extra?'

She laughed and set a bowl in front of me. 'Did you have a good time in Dodge?' she asked.

'Fine,' I said. 'Good liquor. Fast games. Pretty girls. Real pretty girls.'

'Fiddlesticks,' she said. 'I know what you think is pretty. Blond and simpering. You big fool. If you'd killed him over her they'd have put you in jail, at the very least. And just what are you planning to use for an arm when that one gets rotten and falls off? Sit still.'

She got some water and cloth and fixed up my arm where Mr Carmichael's bullet had nicked it.

'Have you been out to your place yet?' she asked.

I shook my head. 'Figure there can't be much out there by now. I'll get after it one of these days.'

'One of these days!' she said. 'You mean when you get tired of strutting around with those big guns and acting dangerous—' She stopped abruptly.

I looked around, and got to my feet. Waco was there in the doorway, and with him was a big man, not as tall as I was, but wider. He was a real whiskery gent, with a mat of black beard you could have used for stuffing a mattress. He wore two gunbelts, crossed, kind of sagging low at the hips.

Waco said, 'You're a fool to sit with your back to the door, Jim. That's the mistake Hickok made, remember? If instead of us it had been somebody like Jack McCall—'

'Who's Jack McCall?' I asked innocently.

'Why, he's the fellow shot Wild Bill in the back....' Waco's face reddened. 'All right, all right. Always kidding me. Dutch, this big joker is my partner, Jim Anderson. Jim, Dutch LeBaron. He's got a proposition for us.'

I tried to think back to where Waco and I had decided to become partners, and couldn't remember the occasion. Well, maybe it happens like that, but it seemed like I should have had some say in it.

'Your partner tells me you're pretty handy with those guns,' LeBaron said, after Martha'd moved off across the room. 'I can use a man like that.'

'For what?' I asked.

'For making some quick money over in New Mexico Territory,' he said.

I didn't ask any fool questions, like whether the money was to be made legally or illegally. 'I'll think about it,' I said.

Waco caught my arm. 'What's to think about? We'll be rich, Jim!'

I said, 'I'll think about it, Waco.'

LeBaron said, 'What's the matter, sonny, are you scared?'

I turned to look at him. He was grinning at me, but his eyes weren't grinning, and his hands weren't too far from those low-slung guns.

I said, 'Try me and see.'

I waited a little. Nothing happened. I walked out of there and got my pony and rode out to the ranch, reaching the place about dawn. I opened the door and stood there, surprised. It looked just about the way it had when the folks were alive, and I half expected to hear Ma yelling at me to beat the dust off outside and not bring it into the house. Somebody had cleaned the place up for me, and I thought I knew who. Well, it certainly was neighbourly of her, I told myself. It was nice to have somebody show a sign they were glad to have me home, even if it was only Martha Butcher.

I spent a couple of days out there, resting up and riding around. I didn't find much stock. It was going to take money to make a going ranch of it again, and I didn't figure my credit at Mr Carmichael's bank was anything to count on. I couldn't help giving some thought to Waco and LeBaron and the proposition they'd put before me. It was funny, I'd think about it most when I had the guns on. I was out back practising with them one day when the stranger rode up.

He was a little, dry, elderly man on a sad-looking white horse he must have hired at the livery stable for not very much, and he wore his gun in front of his left hip with the butt to the right for a cross draw. He didn't make any noise coming up. I'd fired a couple of times before I realized he was there.

'Not bad,' he said when he saw me looking at him. 'Do you know a man named LeBaron, son?'

'I've met him,' I said.

'Is he here?'

'Why should he be here?'

'A bartender in town told me he'd heard you and your sidekick, Smith, had joined up with LeBaron, so I thought you might have given him the use of your place. It would be more comfortable for him than hiding out in the hills.'

'He isn't here,' I said. The stranger glanced toward the house. I started to get mad, but shrugged instead. 'Look around if you want to.'

'In that case,' he said, 'I don't figure I want to.' He glanced towards the target I'd been shooting at, and back to me. 'Killed a man in Dodge, didn't you, son? And then stood real calm and let a fellow here in town fire three shots at you, after which you laughed and pinked him neatly in the leg.'

'I don't recall laughing,' I said. 'And it was two shots, not three.'

'It makes a good story, however,' he said. 'And it is spreading. You have a reputation already, did you know that, Anderson? I didn't come here just to look for LeBaron. I figured I'd like to have a look at you, too. I always like to look up fellows I might have business with later.'

'Business?' I said, and then I saw that he'd taken a tarnished old badge out of his pocket and was pinning it on his shirt. 'Have you a warrant, sir?' I asked.

'Not for you,' he said. 'Not yet.'

He swung the old white horse around and rode off. When he was out of sight, I got my pony out of the corral. It was time I had a talk with Waco. Maybe I was going to join LeBaron and maybe I wasn't, but I didn't much like his spreading it around before it was true.

I didn't have to look for him in town. He came riding to meet me with three companions, all hard ones if I ever saw any.

'Did you see Fenn?' he shouted as he came up. 'Did he come this way?'

'A little old fellow with some kind of a badge?' I said. 'Was that Fenn? He headed back to town, about ten minutes ahead of me. He didn't look like much.'

'Neither does the devil when he's on business,' Waco said. 'Come on, we'd better warn Dutch before he rides into town.'

I rode along with them, and we tried to catch LeBaron on the trail, but he'd already passed with a couple of men. We saw their dust ahead and chased it, but they made it before us, and Fenn was waiting in front of the cantina that was LeBaron's hangout when he was in town.

We saw it all as we came pounding after LeBaron, who dismounted and started into the place, but Fenn came forward, looking small and inoffensive. He was saying something and holding out his hand. LeBaron stopped and shook hands with him, and the little man held on to LeBaron's hand, took a step to the side, and pulled his gun out of that cross-draw holster left-handed, with a kind of twisting motion.

Before LeBaron could do anything with the free hand, the little old man had brought the pistol barrel down across his head. It was as neat and coldblooded a thing as you'd care to see. In an instant, LeBaron was unconscious on the ground, and Old Joe Fenn was covering the two men who'd been riding with him.

Waco Smith, riding beside me, made a sort of moaning sound as if he'd been clubbed himself. 'Get him!' he shouted, drawing his gun. 'Get the dirty sneaking bounty hunter!'

I saw the little man throw a look over his shoulder, but there wasn't much he could do about us with those other two to handle. I guess he hadn't figured us for reinforcements riding in. Waco fired and missed. He never could shoot much, particularly from horseback. I reached out with one of the guns and hit him over the head before he could shoot again. He spilled from the saddle.

I didn't have it all figured out. Certainly it wasn't a very nice thing Mr Fenn had done, first taking a man's hand in friendship and then knocking him unconscious. Still, I didn't figure LeBaron had ever been one for giving anybody a break; and there was something about the old fellow standing there with his tarnished old badge that reminded me of Pa, who'd died wearing a similar piece of tin on his chest. Anyway, there comes a time in a man's life when he's got to make a choice, and that's the way I made mine.

Waco and I had been riding ahead of the others. I turned my pony fast and covered them with the guns as they came charging up—as well as you can cover anybody from a plunging horse. One of them had his pistol aimed to shoot. The left-hand Longley gun went off, and he fell to the ground. I was kind of surprised. I'd never been much at shooting left-handed. The other two riders veered off and headed out of town.

By the time I got my pony quieted down from having that gun go off in his ear, everything was pretty much under control. Waco had disappeared, so I figured he couldn't be hurt much; and the new sheriff was there, old drunken Billy Bates, who'd been elected after Pa's death by the gambling element in town, who hadn't liked the strict way Pa ran things.

'I suppose it's legal,' Old Billy was saying grudgingly. 'But I don't take it kindly, Marshal, your coming here to serve a warrant without letting me know.'

'My apologies, Sheriff,' Fenn said smoothly. 'An oversight, I assure you. Now, I'd like a wagon. He's worth seven hundred and fifty dollars over in New Mexico Territory.'

'No decent person would want that kind of money,' Old Billy said sourly, swaying on his feet.

'There's only one kind of money,' Fenn said. 'Just as there's only one kind of law, even though there's different kinds of men enforcing it.' He looked at me as I came up. 'Much obliged, son.'

'*Por nada*,' I said. 'You get in certain habits when you've had a badge in the family. My daddy was sheriff here once.'

'So? I didn't know that.' Fenn looked at me sharply. 'Don't look like you're making any plans to follow in his footsteps. That's hardly a lawman's rig you're wearing.'

I said, 'Maybe, but I never yet beat a man over the head while I was shaking his hand, Marshal.'

'Son,' he said, 'my job is to enforce the law and maybe make a small profit on the side, not to play games with fair and unfair.' He looked at me for a moment longer. 'Well, maybe we'll meet again. It depends.'

'On what?' I asked.

'On the price,' he said. 'The price on your head.'

'But I haven't got—'

'Not now,' he said. 'But you will, wearing those guns. I know the signs. I've seen them before, too many times. Don't count on having me under obligation to you, when your time comes. I never let personal feelings interfere with business.... Easy, now,' he said to a couple of fellows who were lifting LeBaron, bound hand and foot, into the wagon that somebody had driven up. 'Easy. Don't damage the merchandise. I take pride in delivering them in good shape for standing trial, whenever possible.'

I decided I needed a drink, and then I changed my mind in favour of a cup of coffee. As I walked down the street, leaving my pony at the rail back there, the wagon rolled past and went out of town ahead of me. I was still watching it, for no special reason, when Waco stepped from the alley behind me.

'Jim!' he said. 'Turn around, Jim!'

I turned slowly. He was a little unsteady on his feet, standing there, maybe from my hitting him, maybe from drinking. I thought it was drinking. I hadn't hit him very hard. He'd had time for a couple of quick ones, and liquor always got to him fast.

'You sold us out, you damn traitor!' he cried. 'You took sides with the law!'

'I never was against it,' I said. 'Not really.'

'After everything I've done for you!' he said thickly. 'I was going to make you a great man, Jim, greater than Longley or Hardin or Hickok or any of them. With my brains and your size and speed, nothing could have stopped us! But you turned on me! Do you think you can do it alone? Is that what you're figuring, to leave me behind now that I've built you up to be somebody?'

'Waco,' I said, 'I never had any ambitions to be—'

'You and your medicine guns!' he sneered. 'Let me tell you something. Those old guns are just something I picked up in a pawnshop. I spun a good yarn about them to give you confidence. You were on the edge, you needed a push in the right direction, and I knew once you started wearing a flashy rig like that, with one killing under your belt already, somebody'd be bound to try you again, and we'd be on our way to fame. But as for their being Bill Longley's guns, don't make me laugh!'

I said, 'Waco—'

'They's just metal and wood like any other guns!' he said. 'And I'm going to prove it to you right now! I don't need you, Jim! I'm as good a man as you, even if you laugh at me and make jokes at my expense.... *Are you ready, Jim?*'

He was crouching, and I looked at him, Waco Smith, with whom I'd ridden up the trail and back. I saw that he was no good and I saw that he was dead. It didn't matter whose guns I was wearing, and all he'd really said was that he didn't know whose guns they were. But it didn't matter, they were my guns now, and he was just a little runt who never could shoot for shucks, anyway. He was dead, and so were the others, the ones who'd come after him, because they'd come, I knew that.

I saw them come to try me, one after the other, and I saw them go down before the big black guns, all except the last, the one I couldn't quite make out. Maybe it was Fenn and maybe it wasn't....

I said, 'To hell with you, Waco. I've got nothing against you, and I'm not going to fight you. Tonight or any other time.'

I turned and walked away. I heard the sound of his gun behind me an instant before the bullet hit me. Then I wasn't hearing anything for a while. When I came to, I was in bed, and Martha Butcher was there.

'Jim!' she breathed. 'Oh, Jim . . . !'

She looked real worried, and kind of pretty, I thought, but of course I was half out of my head. She looked even prettier the day I asked her to marry me, some months later, but maybe I was a little out of my head that day, too. Old Man Butcher didn't like it a bit. It seems his fight with Martha had been about her cleaning up my place, and his ordering her to quit and stay away from that young troublemaker, as he'd called me after getting word of all the hell we'd raised up north after delivering his cattle.

He didn't like it, but he offered me a job, I suppose for Martha's sake. I thanked him and told him I was much obliged but I'd just accepted an appointment as Deputy US Marshal. Seems like somebody had recommended me for the job, maybe Old Joe Fenn, maybe not. I got my old gun out of my bedroll and wore it tucked inside my belt when I thought I might need it. It was a funny thing how seldom I had any use for it, even wearing a badge. With that job, I was the first in the neighbourhood to hear about Waco Smith. The news came from New Mexico Territory. Waco and a bunch had pulled a job over there, and a posse had trapped them in a box canyon and shot them to pieces.

I never wore the other guns again. After we moved into the old place, I hung them on the wall. It was right after I'd run against Billy Bates for sheriff and won that I came home to find them gone. Martha looked surprised when I asked about them.

'Why,' she said, 'I gave them to your friend, Mr Williams. He said you'd sold them to him. Here's the money.'

I counted the money, and it was a fair enough price for a pair of second-hand guns and holsters, but I hadn't met any Mr Williams.

I started to say so, but Martha was still talking. She said, 'He certainly had an odd first name, didn't he? Who'd christen anybody Long Williams? Not that he wasn't big enough. I guess he'd be as tall as you, wouldn't he, if he didn't have that trouble with his neck?'

'His neck?' I said.

'Why, yes,' she said. 'Didn't you notice when you talked to him, the way he kept his head cocked to the side? Like this.'

She showed me how Long Williams had kept his head cocked to the side. She looked real pretty doing it, and I couldn't figure how I'd ever thought her plain, but maybe she'd changed. Or maybe

I had. I kissed her and gave her back the gun money to buy something for herself, and went outside to think. Long Williams, William Longley. A man with a wry neck and a man who was hanged twice. It was kind of strange, to be sure, but after a time I decided it was just a coincidence. Some drifter riding by just saw the guns through the window and took a fancy to them.

I mean, if it had really been Bill Longley, if he was alive and had his guns back, we'd surely have heard of him by now down at the sheriff's office, and we never have.

Dorothy M. Johnson

The Man Who Knew the Buckskin Kid

Nobody knows for sure what became of the Buckskin Kid. You can read in books about Western badmen that he killed himself with a pistol shot after he was wounded in a gun battle in Colorado and so avoided capture. Or that a doctor in Wyoming attended a fatally wounded man in his last hours and was pretty sure it was the Buckskin Kid who died then. You can read that he got clean out of the country and went to live in South America. It doesn't matter any more.

Legends grew up along the trails that he had ridden, and as the years slipped by, people who remembered him found that their scanty recollections were of interest to a new generation. An old man can take pride now in having seen the Kid top off a mean bronc on a cold morning half a century ago. Not that he was a better rider than others, but they weren't chiefs of outlaw bands.

Men who were young when the Kid was young grew old in obscurity and now, in their last days, have something to boast about because they saw him once.

John Rossum is one of those obscure old men, but he has never boasted about knowing the Buckskin Kid. A reporter cornered John Rossum at a church social last summer. John didn't know he was a reporter. He just saw this stranger talking to Bill Parker and writing something down.

Bill Parker can't talk without flinging his hands around, and John knew from the hand motions that Bill was telling about the Kid's last train robbery, fifty years ago.

You wouldn't have guessed that John Rossum was amused. His craggy face didn't move a muscle. But he planned what he would tell his wife on the way home:

'There was Bill, telling every detail like he'd been there, and the young feller writing it all down for an eye-witness account.'

Mary would snort, 'I declare, and Bill didn't come out from Iowa till a good ten years later!' and they would chuckle together.

After fifty years, he knew just about what Mary would answer to anything he said. He looked with accustomed admiration towards her; she was bustling with the other women behind the long tables where the bountiful food was set out buffet style.

The stranger was getting restless, listening to Bill Parker go on and on. John Rossum, seeing Bill motion his way, turned quietly towards the door, but half a dozen ranchers blocked the way, talking weather and the price of beef. Courtesy kept him from pushing, so Bill and the young fellow managed to catch him there.

'I was telling him,' Bill said importantly, 'that you knew the Buckskin Kid.'

'I knowed him,' John Rossum answered. 'Lots of people did.'

The young man said, 'Well, thanks,' to Bill Parker, dismissing him. 'How do spell your name, Mr Rossum?'

'I wouldn't care for you to use my name no way,' John said gently. 'I haven't done nothing to get it wrote down for. Travelling by yourself, are you?'

But the young sprout wouldn't have the subject changed.

'This Buckskin Kid Jackson, or Harris, whichever he went by— he hid out around here, I understand. Did you know him then?'

The Kid had been a killer four times over, and, in John Rossum's opinion, knowing him was nothing to boast about, but there was such a thing as truth. And the memory of even the Buckskin Kid deserved justice. John Rossum spoke for truth and justice:

'He wasn't one to hide from nobody. Take any old broken-down cabin, and somebody'll tell you that was the Kid's hideout. But he didn't have to hide. He wasn't afraid of nobody.'

The reporter looked pleased. 'You were here then?' he insisted.

Unable to avoid answering, unwilling to lie, John Rossum said, 'I was here.'

He glanced over at Mary, behind the long tables, and knew that she was aware he was in mild trouble. But she couldn't leave there; she was ladling out baked beans.

'What did the Kid look like?' the reporter asked.

John Rossum tried to remember. 'Just ordinary, far as I recall. His brother Ben was skinny, but the Kid just looked ordinary.'

'Bill Parker was telling me somebody put a fence around Ben's grave,' the reporter remarked. 'Thought I'd go get a picture of it tomorrow. I'd like to have you in the picture, Mr Rossum. Okay with you?'

'I wouldn't wish to have my picture made,' John Rossum said firmly.

'Do you think the Kid went to South America?' the reporter

demanded. 'Mr Parker says he knows people who say they got postcards from him there.'

'I always thought he went there,' John Rossum said. Meticulously honest, he added, 'I never got no postcards.'

'I met a man yesterday who said Pinkerton's Detective Agency was still looking for the Kid in 1914, when he was supposed to be long dead.'

'I don't know what became of him,' John Rossum said. 'I suppose he'd be dead by this time. He'd be pridnear eighty now.'

The reporter got a sly grin on his face as he asked, 'You knew his girl friend, I suppose?'

'I seen her once or twice. Never could see why she took up with the Kid.' (Couldn't understand why he took up with her, either, John Rossum thought; she was real plain. But gallantry did not permit him to say that.)

'She lit out about the same time he did, I heard.'

'I heard the same,' John Rossum agreed.

He wished the reporter was willing to talk about something important, like Russia or how jet planes worked. The problems of the present concerned John Rossum mightily. But this young fellow was interested only in some old-time outlaws.

Mary was getting away from the beans. Nobody was in line any more. She patted her hair as she came towards him, and he noted with relief that she had on her managing expression.

She managed fine, too. She nodded at the young man and dismissed him with a motherly smile.

John nodded politely to the reporter, who said with a grin, 'I don't suppose you ever rode with the Kid, Mr Rossum?'

'No,' John Rossum answered. 'I never did.' He added without rancour, 'Not so long ago, you could have got in trouble for asking a question like that.' Then he went with Mary and ate pie he didn't want at all.

'The other ladies will clear things away,' she said. 'We can go now, unless you want to stay.'

'Got nothing to stay for, unless you do,' John answered. He thought she wanted to, but she said not. That was Mary for you— willing to leave early because she knew he would like to get away. There never was a woman like Mary. Or if there was, he hoped she had a man who deserved her.

Driving home in the old pickup, steering along rutted roads, his conscience hurt with an ache to which he was long accustomed.

He and Mary didn't talk, because there was no need for it. Mary understood that he wished to think.

He remembered the Buckskin Kid, after Ben was dead and after the Kid came back and killed Ben's killer. The Kid was at his peak then. He owned the world, or anyway he roamed free in a piece of Montana about a hundred miles across.

And in those days John Rossum didn't own a thing but a bay horse and a saddle.

Johnny Rossum was young then and unsure, just a drifting cowboy, didn't know what he wanted of the world and wouldn't have known how to get it anyway. The Buckskin Kid told him once, 'By damn, Johnny, the trouble with you is you think too much.'

Young John Rossum answered, 'Guess you're right, Kid, but how's a man going to stop?'

'Here's one way,' the Kid said, grinning, and pushed a bottle along the bar.

'That won't stop a man from thinking for very long, though,' Johnny commented. 'And anyway, there's so many things to think about.'

'Besides women and money, what is there?' the Kid challenged, so seriously that Johnny laughed out loud and said, 'See, you're doing it, too.'

Women and money—the Buckskin Kid was partly right. Johnny did a lot of thinking about them, or to be exact, he thought about one young woman and how he had no money. Mary Browning had other admirers, but Johnny thought—when he was feeling optimistic—that she sort of favoured him. His rivals had what Johnny lacked: some land, some cattle, a roof, even if the roof was only sod on a shack.

Mary was better off at home with her pa than she would be with Johnny Rossum. But she was nineteen, old enough to marry, and she was not indispensable to her pa, for she had a sister two years younger who could cook. Somebody would sure enough stake a claim to Mary Browning before very long.

Johnny Rossum wasn't exactly courting her. He just stopped by her pa's place whenever he was in the neighbourhood—say twenty miles away. Sometimes she favoured him by going for a walk with him along the river.

'Do we always have to have your horse along?' she demanded once.

Johnny glanced back in some surprise at the horse he was leading.

'Shucks, no. Could leave him in your pa's yard. You don't like having the horse along, huh?' That seemed important to him.

Mary thought his feelings were hurt. She reached up and scratched around the horse's ears.

'He's a nice horse. I don't mind if he comes along. I just wonder why you bring him when we're only out for a few minutes on foot.'

There was something for Johnny to think about, and he thought hard. When he got the answer, it was so silly it embarrassed him.

'I'm not used to going afoot, that's all, I guess. If my boss was to order me to, I'd ask for my time. But as long as a man's leading his horse, he ain't afoot, really. Now ain't that silly! But it's true,' said honest Johnny Rossum.

'And now I made a fool of myself admitting that,' he suggested. 'Maybe you'll say why you don't like the horse's company?'

Mary Browning giggled. 'I always think if I made a quick move you'd swing up on him and ride for your life, that's all,' she said.

'Quick move? You think I'm scared you'll make a quick move?' John Rossum said triumphantly. 'I'll show you what a quick move is!' and grabbed her and kissed her good while she struggled and laughed and her hair came loose, pretty Mary Browning.

She had no cause for struggle, having invited that kissing, but it was part of the game, and they both knew it. Johnny knew, too, that it was only a game. That was the kind of kissing a man could give a girl at a party, laughing and funning, even with her folks and her relatives and the preacher looking on.

Riding back to the ranch where he worked, he dreamed idly of the kiss he had never given Mary Browning and maybe never would, the solemn, earnest kind, with sighing but no laughter. Mary couldn't afford to take a serious kiss from a man who was only a cowboy. Cowboys did not marry.

We got no homes, Johnny told himself.

He had a roof over his head when he was at the headquarters ranch. He slept with two other cowboys in a sod bunkhouse. Mostly the roof kept the rain off.

'But it ain't my roof, damn it,' he said out loud.

A week later, he didn't even have another man's roof, because the boss insulted him and he had to quit the job. Even making allowances for the fact that the boss was a tenderfoot, an Eastern fellow who had inherited the cattle, what he did could not be overlooked or excused. He did it right in front of the other hands, too.

The boss asked, 'Johnny, did you look for the new bulls over beyond the red butte?'

Johnny had been told to find those bulls and move them, and he had done so. If he had failed, he would have said so. To be asked about it was to be insulted, although Johnny was not unduly sensitive. So he did what unwritten law required.

'I carried out your orders, Mr Smith,' he said gently. 'Now I'll have to ask for my time.'

So he collected the pay he had coming, packed up his war sack with what every cowboy called his 'forty years' gatherings' whether he had lived forty years or not, and headed sadly for town.

It was only ten miles out of his way to stop at Mary's, so he did, but he didn't stay long. She had company, a rancher named Tip Warren, who spoke politely but then ignored Johnny Rossum, as much as to say, 'With Mary Browning I've got the inside track. You count so little that I won't even waste time cutting you out.'

And Mary paid much attention to Tip Warren. It never dawned on Johnny that she might be trying to make him jealous. He didn't feel jealous. He just felt as if something he hadn't expected to get anyway had been moved a little farther out of reach.

Tip Warren remarked while they were sitting around, 'I'm short-handed. One man broke his leg, another one lit out ahead of the sheriff. Guess I can pick up a couple of hands in town though.'

That was Johnny's cue to say Tip didn't need to go into town, but he didn't say it. He wasn't figuring to work for a man who was courting his girl. Not if he starved, he wouldn't do that.

So he went on into Fork City right after supper, turned his horse into the small pasture back of the livery stable, and bedded himself down on the hay by permission of the hostler.

It was pure accident, next morning, that he ran into the Buckskin Kid. The Kid was affable except when he was roaring drunk, and when he was in Fork City he didn't get drunk. He watched his step there and usually didn't come in unless he was pretty sure the sheriff was at the other end of the county. That was how they got along, with a kind of truce that nobody talked about or maybe even thought about.

Johnny Rossum wasn't afraid of the Kid, but didn't like him much. He had an idea he might glimpse blood on the Kid's hands if he stared long enough, but he never stared at the Buckskin Kid, and neither did anyone else. In brief, Johnny's attitude was just about normal—he respected the Kid as a successful man and steered clear when he could do so without being conspicuous.

But the Kid liked Johnny Rossum, as most people did, and admired his brains, which other people ignored.

So in the saloon that morning, where Johnny was hanging around in the hope that some cattleman would come in who wanted to hire a hand, the Kid friendlied up to him. Johnny valued his health, so he friendlied back.

'I been thinking about you,' the Kid said, 'since I seen you last. A man that can think is kind of useful sometimes, know what I mean?'

'Sure,' agreed Johnny.

The Kid saw that he hadn't got the point. 'A thinking man could be useful to me, I mean,' he hinted.

Johnny got the idea and answered, 'I ain't very useful to anybody.'

The Kid set down his glass. 'I'll be out at Mamie's this evening with some of the boys, if you was to come by.'

There it was, a direct invitation to a man who could think, an invitation to join up with a man of action. And Johnny had nothing to lose, the way he looked at his life right then.

So that evening he rode out to Mamie's thinking hard. Once he pulled up his horse and thought hard while sitting in the saddle, with half a mind to turn back toward obscure respectability. What moved him on towards the meeting with the Kid was not any final decision of his own but the restlessness of the horse. When the horse started ahead in a tentative kind of way, Johnny growled, 'Well, all right, if you're so anxious.'

He hollered cautiously in Mamie's yard and didn't dismount until the door opened. It wasn't the Kid in the lighted doorway. But the man said, 'Git down, we're waiting,' and as Johnny came up to him he saw it was Windy Witherspoon. The others in there were Deaf Parker and Gus Graves, and, of course, Mamie was there.

Afterwards, it struck Johnny as funny that while he sat with the Kid's gang, planning a train robbery, Mamie tiptoed around with a plate of layer cake and glasses of lemonade. The Kid finally told her to stop it and go on with her packing if she intended to get out of the country while the going was good.

'She's going to go visit her brother's folks in Minneapolis,' the Kid told Johnny with a wink. So Johnny always supposed that wherever she did go, certainly not Minneapolis, the Kid met her there later.

The Kid said, with cake frosting on his mustache, 'There's a currency shipment coming through, Johnny. You want to throw in with us?'

The other men stared at Johnny Rossum through the smoke of good cigars. Deaf Parker died of gunshot wounds in Wyoming. Windy died of the same in Nevada, Gus of old age in prison, and nobody know for sure how the Kid ended, or where. But that night, none of them knowing how they'd finish up, those famous outlaws sat in Mamie's cabin, waiting for Johnny Rossum to say something.

'I come, didn't I?' he growled. Then his conscience hurt him. 'Whose money is it?'

The Kid shrugged. 'Who cares? The bank's getting it—or they think they are. Maybe the railroad gets held responsible. You got a soft spot in your heart for banks and railroads?'

'Guess not,' Johnny admitted. He had had little contact with either of them. 'It ain't like robbing folks. Where are we going to do it?'

Gus grunted, 'That's what you're supposed to help figure out, Mr Brains.'

Johnny stuck his chin out and demanded, 'You willing I should?' and Gus nodded.

The Kid said, 'Not very far from here. We never pulled a train job around here, so they won't expect it. Means we can't hang around here afterwards, of course, because we'd get the credit even if somebody else done it. But you could stay if you want to take the chance. If everything goes all right.'

Johnny Rossum drew in a deep breath. Get me some cattle with my share of the take, maybe get my girl too, settle down and never do another wicked thing. Where'll I tell her the money came from? Figure that out after I get it. Got brains, ain't I?

'The boys and me, we don't want to be seen investigating along the railroad,' the Kid explained. 'But I got two, three places in mind. You go look, make plans, come back and tell me, and we'll all work out the details, if you're still game.'

'All right,' Johnny said, 'go ahead and talk.'

He was a jobless cowboy; nobody cared where he went. If anyone saw him go for a swim under a certain bridge, nobody connected it with the train robbery that became history. He had himself a good bath in the river and lazied around for a while, all alone. He took some rough measurements, by eye, of how far away the cottonwood grove was and just where the brush was thick, and he noted where there were some railroad ties that would come in handy.

He loafed around on the prairie for a couple of days, sizing things up at the places the Kid had mentioned, and one night he went out to Mamie's to talk to the boys.

He drew a diagram. 'Put ties on the track right there. Not so's to wreck the train, but so the engineer will see 'em and stop. That'll bring the express car to right about here. The man that's going to cover the engine crew can hide under the bridge till the time comes. Others behind the tie pile on the north. Horses can be waiting in them cottonwoods, handy for the getaway. The conductor'll come running when the train stops, and the man at the head end can get a gun on him right away.'

The boys argued every foot of the layout to make sure the plan was solid. The Kid asked them, 'Sound all right to you?'

They nodded, and Johnny saw they were grinning.

'That's the exact place we picked out ourselves,' the Kid told Johnny. 'We wasn't so ignorant as we let on.'

Johnny wasn't mad when he learned they had just been testing him out. He began to think maybe he had talent.

'You're going to hold the horses,' the Buckskin Kid told him. 'This ain't like a bank job, where the horse holder is liable to get shot at. Nobody's going to see you in the cottonwoods, and we might need some covering fire from there. Got a rifle, boy?'

Johnny nodded. He had never hit a human being with his rifle, though he had tried once when an Indian was trying to steal a cow.

'When I find out the day,' the Kid said, 'I'll send you word. Just hang around town.'

In the next few days, while the Kid was waiting to find out when the currency would be coming through, Johnny tried to get the feel of being an outlaw. He couldn't tell yet what it would be like, but he decided one thing: no dirty outlaw was good enough for Mary Browning.

A man's got to say good-bye to his girl, he told himself. Without letting her know it's good-bye. Got to have one last look at her, to remember; got to hint that he's going away for a while. She'll catch on, finally, that it's forever. And likely she won't care much anyway.

So he went to see Mary one last time.

'Leaving the country pretty soon,' he said casually. 'Man might want me to drive some horses to Canada. Wants me to work for him there anyway.'

'Canada?' Mary repeated, as if the border were a thousand miles away instead of fifty. She didn't talk much, seemed mad at him when he left. He was sorry about that but thought it was probably for the best.

As he rode back to Fork City, he felt bad enough to cry.

One day the Kid sent him word, and they met secretly.

'Monday afternoon,' the Kid told him. 'We'll be away from here before that. Separately. You go before daylight Monday. Looking for a job somewhere, something like that. It don't matter what your reason is as long as it sounds good.'

'Nobody'll care,' Johnny admitted. 'I'll grouch and gab to the hostler about going to Canada.'

'All right with me.' The Kid hesitated. 'I'm giving you the easy part. You know that, don't you?'

'I didn't ask for no favours,' Johnny reminded him. 'But I'm grateful. I thought maybe you were making me horse holder because I'm green and might get in the way doing anything else.'

The Kid barked a laugh. 'Yessir, you got brains. My brother Ben, now, I used to have him hold the horses because he wasn't smart enough for anything else. But for you it's a kind of apprenticeship. And you get the same split the other boys do.'

He slapped Johnny on the shoulder when they parted, and Johnny kept imagining he felt the mark of the outlaw's hand on him for quite a while afterwards. When he was out on the street, he wondered if it showed.

Sunday, he grouched and gabbed to the hostler, who agreed things were pretty quiet and a man might have a better chance to get work if he hit north. So Johnny put his forty years' gatherings in his war sack before he went to bed in the hay.

He got up while it was still dark and walked out carrying his saddle. Nobody saw him, and if anybody had, they would not have guessed that he was scared or that he wished he wasn't going to rob a train.

He never did rob it, either.

The Buckskin Kid's gang got $40 000 out of the express car safe, but Johnny Rossum wasn't with them, because he couldn't find his horse in the pasture.

The horse just wasn't there. Someone had opened the gate.

He squinted all around in the darkness and searched over every foot of the ground, but there was no horse in there.

A man couldn't rent a horse if he said he was taking it across the border. And if he just took one, he'd be a horse thief, beneath contempt. Money belonged to banks, but horses belonged to people. A man had to draw the line somewhere.

That was a bad day for Johnny, because he thought a lot of that horse. He was glooming around town when the train robbery took place miles away.

Word of the robbery came about suppertime. It spread along the telegraph wires and caught up with the sheriff. He came tearing back and began organizing posses, cussing a blue streak at the Buckskin Kid, and paid no attention when Johnny tried to report that his horse was strayed.

So when the sheriff said a few minutes later, 'I want you in a posse, young feller,' Johnny told him to go to hell and take the posse with him.

Somebody picked up the stray horse on Tuesday in time for the sheriff to requisition it, along with every other four-legged animal big enough to cinch a saddle on, for the posses that went riding out in every direction.

They never got the Buckskin Kid, though, and Johnny Rossum never saw him or heard from him again.

While the posses were riding around hell for leather, chasing bandits, Johnny went out to see Mary Browning. Having no horse to ride, he walked all ten miles of it. When she came out to meet him, she had the most startled look on her face.

'You mean to say you came all the way on foot?' she demanded. 'Just to see me? Oh, Johnny!'

That was the time he first kissed her the solemn, earnest way, with sighing and no laughter, right there in front of her pa's house with her sister peeking out the window. Then he pulled away and shook his head.

'A while back,' he said, 'I didn't have a thing but my horse and saddle. Right now, I ain't even got the horse. But I come to tell you . . .'

'Yes?' she whispered, trying to snuggle into his arms again. 'Say it, Johnny, say it.'

'I come to tell you,' he finished lamely, 'that I wish I was rich!'

She knew, miraculously, exactly what he meant, but he always regretted he hadn't said it fancier.

There wasn't any serious problem after that, really. They built a shack on her pa's place, and Johnny worked for him, and after a few years he and Mary had cattle of their own and four children and a mighty good life.

Fifty years later, the evil he had meant to do still plagued him. He hadn't earned that good life at all.

The lane to the home place was half a mile ahead when he said urgently, 'I got to tell you something,' and the woman who had been his wife for half a century answered, 'Hmm?'

He hated to do it, hated to have her know, even now, how weak he had been, how wicked he had meant to be.

'That fellow talking about the Buckskin Kid,' he said hurriedly. 'I got to thinking there's something I have to tell you. I almost— that is, I would have—well, that last big holdup the Kid pulled, I would have been in it if my horse hadn't strayed.'

Mary sounded as shocked as he had expected.

'John Rossum,' she said, 'I can hardly believe it!'

'It's true,' he sighed.

'I never suspected that,' she said, and was silent for a while. 'Now I can tell you something you never knew. You were acting so mysterious in those days, I thought you had another girl on the string, in Canada, maybe, or that Mamie.'

'Mamie!' John Rossum gulped.

'I thought there was some girl, anyway,' his wife told him. 'So I rode into town and let down that gate and spooked your horse out of that pasture myself, if you want to know it, so's you couldn't get away easy!'

He felt a wild chuckle welling up inside him, but before he could answer Mary said something else:

'You know, I was bound and determined to have you. If you had gone off with those bandits, and if you'd asked me—well, I'd have gone along.'

He said, 'Why, Mary Rossum!' and took a quick, horrified glance at this woman whom he suddenly felt he didn't know at all.

Dorothy M. Johnson

Blanket Squaw

The new road to High Valley was opened this past summer, and everybody in Okanasket County turned out to celebrate. Helga Jacobsen, our art teacher, went to the canyon mouth with me in my car to watch the parade. She's so crazy about our part of the state of Washington that she came back before school started.

Behind the band—a good distance behind, so they'd have room to make a grand entrance—came a bunch of young Indians, most of them on their best paint ponies, worth—they claim—a dollar a spot. The boys were all painted up and more than half naked, and they tore out of the woods into the sunshine, leaning low and shrieking in a way that no doubt curdled their own blood. It just sounded like the last day of school to me.

Helga, sitting on the running board, snapped a picture and remarked, 'Aren't they having fun!'

'Get off that running board!' I yelped. 'The noble red men can't stop!'

I swung the door open and got her into the car just in time. The ponies went past us in a thunder of hoofs and a cloud of dust. The youngsters were trying to pull up, but there wasn't space enough for all those excited horses. Those in front got clear, but the last half dozen piled up right beside my car, with a thumping of boys' bare heels on ponies' bare ribs, and a hullabaloo of yelling, some of which sounded just plain scared. One horse went down.

The rider, a gangling Indian boy wearing swimming trunks, with red and yellow paint streaked over his bare skin, automatically curled up with his arms around his head for protection. Someone caught his pony and another boy helped him to his feet. He shook his head dizzily, but he wore a valiant grin.

'Are you all right?' I called. . . . 'Bring him into the car, boys.'

'Naw,' he said. 'The paint might come off on your cushions.' But he did condescend to sit on the running board to watch the rest of the show. He had what a medical report would probably call multiple abrasions, and blood was running from a long scraped place on his leg, but he studiously ignored it.

I wondered who he was, because he seemed to know me, but I had never seen quite so much of any Indian boy before, and I didn't recognize him in all his bare skin and war paint. He had a complicated design on his face that made him look positively homicidal.

The next contingent was filing down out of the canyon with more dignity. These were the old braves, gaudy and proud, some of them wearing the great nodding war bonnets they had inherited from their grandfathers, along with a great tradition. Dark-faced and impassive, riding as if they did not know they had horses under them, they filed down singly so as to make a more impressive show. There were not many of these older men; they could not afford to ride in pairs, because that would have made the line too short. Some of them wore their hair in thin grey braids.

The painted youngster on the running board emitted a piercing whistle of greeting, but not one of the older men turned his head.

Helga was taking pictures as fast as she could work her camera, talking happily to herself. All she said to me for ten minutes was 'Here, hold this,' while she changed a film.

The old men were followed by the younger men, not quite so gaudy as their elders, because when grandpa owns the feathers, grandpa wears the feathers. The rest have to get along with what they can rig up.

'Oh, there come the squaws,' remarked Helga. I gave her a jab in the ribs, thinking the youngster on the running board might not like that word used to describe his own relatives.

The women came two by two, but leading them, one woman came alone, a heavy woman, wearing a black kerchief over her head and a grey and black striped shawl. She alone wore dull raiment, but she had dignity and self-possession. She rode a bony grey horse, and she sat in a chairlike saddle that had every visible inch covered with heavy, gaudy patterns of beadwork. She wore at least three petticoats—there were that many showing. I saw her face as she went by—a broad, dark face, unsmiling, distant, wrinkled and serene.

'Who was the one in front?' I asked the boy on the running board.

'Her? My grandmother,' he answered.

'A great help you are,' I told him. 'What's your grandmother's grandson's name?'

His grin went clear to his ears. 'Didn't know me, eh? I'm Joe Hawk.'

'Oh, my land! I see you in school five days a week—or should, young man—and didn't know you with your war paint on. What's your grandma's name?'

'Mary,' he said. Then, dismissing the distaff side of the family, he added boastfully, 'My great-grandfather was a medicine man.'

Something clicked in my memory. 'Her name is Mary. Mary . . . Waters?'

'I got cousins named Waters,' he reasoned it out. 'So I guess her name might 'a' been that before she married grandpa. The fellers want me, Miss Bunny. G'bye now.' He galloped off.

'Did you get a picture of the squaw on the grey horse?' I asked Helga, who was aiming at an oncoming cowboy.

She shook her head. 'I'm running short of film. She wasn't very special, anyway.'

'You wouldn't know,' I said. 'You never knew Mary Waters.'

'Oh, here come the guests of honour!' she exclaimed. 'Look!'

They were riding in the old Concord coach that is kept in the firehouse and brought out for big occasions. The band, congregated on the hill behind us, began to blare a welcome to those men, the two state senators, who rode inside the coach and gravely waved their hats to the crowd. They had helped fight for the road from High Valley to the highway, and they deserved honour. But the band was playing for white-bearded Steve Morris, too, the man who had spent more than forty discouraging years bringing prosperity to his valley.

Steve Morris rode high above the people, on the driver's seat of the Concord coach. He wore a battered grey hat, pushed back so he could see, not tilted as young men wear their hats. Grizzled old Two Line Tooker, sitting beside him, drove the four horses.

That was the way I saw them, finally—Mary Waters and Steve Morris—a quarter of a mile apart on a brave new road in a bright procession, but a lifetime apart really, with a racial difference between them, and a decision dividing them forever.

I grew up with Mary Waters, the Indian girl, on a ranch that's been deserted now for a good many years. The buildings have fallen in now, and the wild cayuses can find shelter in bitter weather where my folks used to sit beside the heating stove that had been freighted up from Wenatchee by boat, long before the railroad came.

Mary's father worked for my father sometimes, and her mother helped my mother, and Mary kept an eye on me. She was five years older. I was afraid of her father, because people said he was a medicine man. I don't suppose he really was. He was stern and silent, a bulky man with long black braids dangling from under his hat. His trousers always seemed ready to slide off him, and his shirt hung over them.

Mary's mother was a blanket squaw. She wore my mother's old dresses, but when she wore them they looked baggy and unkempt. She usually wore a shawl. What my mother asked her to do around the house, she did, and nothing more. When she finished a task, she simply squatted down on the floor and rested her stooped back against the wall until Ma told her what to do next.

Sometimes the whole family lived in our bunkhouse. Sometimes they lived in a tepee. And sometimes they disappeared between darkness and daylight, no matter if Pa had sheds to be mended and cattle to be driven, no matter if Ma had canning to do and wanted someone around to keep me out from under foot. After a while our Indians would come back and go to work again, and that was all there was to it.

Pa used to grumble about it, but Ma would say, 'What kind of help did you expect in the savage wilderness?' Ma never relished being a pioneer.

I remember the first time I ever saw Mary Waters. Ma said to her, 'Take good care of the baby,' and Mary took me by the hand. We played down by the creek. Our game was mostly a business of crouching in the brush and saying 'Listen!' I don't know what Mary was hearing, I heard nothing but the usual woodsy sounds.

Ma mourned that there was no school for me; and so, when I was about six, she undertook to teach me herself. While she was about it, she taught Mary, too, because otherwise I saw no sense in sitting still. Mary learned so fast that she had to have a book more advanced than mine. That kept me humping because I was jealous, so we both went faster than the public schools would let anybody go now. We didn't waste any time colouring squirrel pictures and making papers chains; we just learned.

Mary taught me, down by the creek, to braid horsehair and sew beads and to talk the Chinook jargon—a mixture of French, English and Indian words. I've forgotten most of it now.

When she was fifteen and I was ten, her older brother came back from somewhere with another tough young buck.

'Expect we'll be losing our nursemaid soon,' Pa said one night at supper. 'I think that young buck that came with her brother is talking business with the old man. She's marrying age.'

I sat with my mouth open, ready to cry. Ma's eyes widened and she put down her fork with a clatter. 'Do you mean to tell me these savages marry off their daughters at fifteen?' she demanded. 'Carl, I won't have it!'

'You can't very well stop it,' he answered reasonably. 'How would you like to have somebody tell you when you could marry off Beulah here?'

I got ready to slide under the table. I didn't even like boys and here were my own parents planning on having me marry somebody!

'But you can't have Mary settling down to be just another squaw!' Ma wailed. 'You'll have to do something about it.' She began to cut her meat again, as if everything had been settled.

Pa was a patient man. 'She's Injun,' he said.

'She's bright,' said Ma. She glanced up at him. 'It would be nice if you'd send her away to school,' she remarked. 'People do it sometimes. But of course you couldn't afford it.'

'I've got some influence,' Pa growled.

'You surely haven't got that much,' scoffed Ma.

Pa put his fork down hard. 'Who says I haven't?'

That was how Mary Waters went back East to school for two years. Ma went on teaching me at home.

I don't know what school Mary went to. She must have known she had not much time to be there, and she must have used that little time well. I remember the day she came back. Ma wanted Pa to go down and get her with the wagon, and I sulked and wept because he wouldn't.

'Let her folks get her,' he insisted. 'They can ride down and take an extra horse for her. I don't want to have to wait around for the stage and then ride back with an Indian girl in the wagon. It wouldn't look right.'

He didn't win that argument, but neither did Ma. He simply didn't go.

Mary and I would ride up in the hills, I planned. I would let her shoot the old rifle Pa had given me over Ma's frenzied protests. We would hide down by the creek and say, 'Listen!' And perhaps, being now twelve, I might find out what it was that I was supposed to hear.

I would rush out the door, I planned, and clamber up behind Mary's saddle as soon as she arrived; I'd grasp her around the waist, and we would ride off pell-mell into the coulees and yell to raise the echoes.

But I didn't even hear them come. Suddenly there was a movement out in the yard, and I saw a lady swinging down off a horse, with two Indians getting off theirs. The lady turned her back on the Indians and came straight on to the house. She rapped, although the door was open, and stood there smiling.

Her black hair was in two braids around her head, and she wore a long blue dress. (Ma almost cried when she told Pa about it later. 'Carl, if you could have seen how wrinkled her pretty dress was! She shouldn't have had to ride up on a pony. You should have taken the wagon. She expected it.' But Pa clamped his jaw and answered, 'Injuns ride horses.') I was dumb-struck. I couldn't even say hello.

'Why, Mary!' my mother greeted her. 'Do come in. Beulah has made a cake to celebrate.'

'Thank you,' Mary said. She came in and remained standing.

Ma never asked an Indian to sit down unless there was work to be done that required it, but she looked quickly around and then at Mary in her blue dress. 'Have a chair,' she said.

'Thank you,' Mary answered. She sat down like a lady.

Ma must have realized then what she had done. There was no way she could undo it. When you have made a lady, you must treat her like a lady. Poor Ma, she always tried to make one of me, but the results she got with Mary didn't give her much satisfaction. It was school-teaching that made a lady out of Beulah—if anything ever did.

Mary ate her piece of cake with a fork, from a saucer. I surreptitiously wiped frosting off my fingers onto my petticoat and picked up the fork I had ignored.

They talked about Mary's trip, and her school, and the weather. What they did not talk about, what they dared not talk about, was, 'Well Mary, and what do you plan to do now?'

Next day Mary and I got acquainted again. She wore her old clothes, hand-me-downs, but she had washed them, although she had no way to iron them. She wore them in a temporary kind of way, as if this part of her life were an interlude that would pass.

We walked down by the creek, talking. I stooped in the brush by the water and whispered, 'Listen!'

Mary listened, shook her head and smiled brightly. 'To what?' she answered. So I still don't know.

Very quietly, without speaking to my parents about it, Mary

rode down to Okanasket one day, carrying her blue dress in a bundle on the saddle. In the grove by the river she took off her Indian clothing and put on the blue dress. Then she went into town on foot and applied for a job teaching school. She applied at the store. Then she went from house to house. When it was getting dark, she put on her Indian clothes again and rode home on her pony.

Pa was angry about it, when people told him later. Ma looked as if she wanted to cry.

A week later, Mary came softly to the back door and said to my mother, 'I've come to say good-bye for a while, Mrs Bunny. My aunt is cooking for a construction crew out past Okanasket, and I'm going to help her.'

It never occurred to Ma to shake hands when they parted, but I saw that Mary had her right hand ready.

Ma told Pa all about Mary's job. He was more interested in the construction crew than in the cookhouse help.

'That's a big thing they're doing up there,' he said. 'High Valley, Steve Morris calls the territory. Thinks if he can just get water up there, he can make something of it for settlers. Smart fellow, Steve is. Puts his whole heart into anything he undertakes. He's a dreamer though.'

'Steve Morris?' my mother inquired.

'Young widower. He wants to open up that valley. I don't know why. There's plenty others. Going to build a dam and an irrigation system—says he can't wait for the Government to do it. Got some settlers up there already. You know the place, Effie—you go through that dark canyon past the Riley ranch.'

'Oh, yes. My, I wonder how Esther Riley is. I haven't seen her in months.'

For once I was wise enough not to announce pugnaciously that I wanted to go visit the Rileys. For two or three days I asked pensive questions about them. I even suggested that Mrs Riley had looked to me like a sick lady, which she certainly had not. But Ma got worried enough to decide that a little visit would do us both good.

Having found that pensiveness worked at home, I tried it on Mrs Riley. She sent one of her boys to tell Mary Waters to come to see me, and Mary came.

She wore her Indian clothes still, in the same temporary way as when she had first put them on after her return. She was gracious to me—not condescending, but gracious as any older girl may be to a younger one. We ran foot races, which I never won, and we rode bareback, with a hackamore instead of a bridle. We had fun.

After Mary went back to wherever she had come from, I stole up to the back door and heard Mrs Riley talking to my mother.

'There's been too much talk,' she was saying. 'Her aunt made her quit working up at the dam. She's staying with relatives now, over the hills somewhere, and they won't let her see Steve.'

'Is he a nice man?' my mother inquired.

'Fine man, and nobody would be surprised if he got married again. But he's not the type to be a squaw man. Even if he does turn into one, he's still not the type, if you understand what I mean.'

My mother made clicking sounds denoting interest and dismay.

'The girl's own folks wouldn't like it, either,' Mrs Riley said. 'They're good people in their own way.'

'You never had to put up with them or you might not think so,' Ma argued.

'I've put up with others, and I know good Injuns when I see 'em,' Mrs Riley insisted. 'Well, that Steve is a dreamer, and he'll dream himself into trouble one way or another, I suppose.'

I heard Mr Riley telling later about the dam, in a masterfully masculine way, as if he didn't expect women to understand.

'It ain't such great shucks as a dam,' he explained, 'but Steve thinks if he builds it as good as he can, he can convince the Government that the valley needs a real good one. I don't think he's much of a dam builder, but it's none of my business. Hear they're going to let the water on it one of these days soon. That'll be the big day for Steve Morris.'

'Could we go up and watch?' Mrs Riley pleaded, with the hunger of all women in the wilderness who do not have many pleasant disturbances to interrupt the hard routine.

'Sure,' Mr Riley promised expansively. 'Unless old Steve keeps it a secret. Next time I see him, I'll ask him when it will be.'

Mary came down to visit me two or three times during the week we visited the Rileys. She had changed her attitude toward my mother and Mrs Riley. She no longer stood with her shoulders straight; she no longer looked them straight in the eye as an equal. She stood a little stooped, looking at the floor. They treated her more gently, and with less bewilderment, because of that. I know now that she did it for that reason, because she had a plan.

Hesitantly she confronted my mother and spoke to my mother's shoes. 'Could we—Beulah thought it would be nice—go on a long ride and maybe take a picnic lunch if there was anything to spare? Anyway, maybe just a sandwich for Beulah, and I could bring something for myself?'

Ma tapped a finger against her front teeth, considering. 'Why, if you'd promise to take good care of Beulah, I think it would be all right, Mary. That is, if Mr Riley can spare a pony.'

'Oh, I can bring another pony,' Mary promised.

And so, to my unbounded surprise, we went the next day for a long ride into the woods. The whole thing, including the part about 'Beulah thought it would be nice', was a surprise to me. Mary had made that up, and had said nothing about it to me in advance.

Mary did not ask me where I wanted to go. We rode over the hills, out of sight of the house, and then doubled back by a circuitous route and went over more and steeper hills, through the woods for a long way, until we came out in a clearing. At one side the plateau dropped off so that you could see the darkness of treetops below. Down there men were working with horses and lumber and logs. There were shacks there too. Out of one of them came an Indian woman carrying something, which she threw away.

'Get back,' Mary whispered. 'That's my aunt. We don't want her to see us. We're playing a game.'

'What do we pretend now?' I demanded.

'You're a spy,' she said. 'And I'm the captain of the army. You have to deliver a message for me, and if you're caught, they'll shoot you. You have to find a tall man with brown hair and beard and blue eyes, and say, when nobody's listening, "Mary's where the trail forks." Do you understand?'

'Sure. But does the man know about the game?'

'He'll play it,' she promised.

I skulked through the brush and lay in wait near where the men were working until I singled out the tall, brown-bearded man where nobody else would hear me. When I whispered, 'Mary's where the trail forks,' he turned around, startled; then he smiled. When I repeated it, he stopped smiling and answered, 'Well. All right.'

When he found her, she was standing proudly, with her head up, even in her Indian clothes. I saw the sun on her black hair and his brown head. I saw him take both her hands in his.

Then Mary saw me and pushed his hands away. 'Go watch for the enemy,' she warned me, and I was glad to go.

I found no enemy attacking party, but there was a nice boy working with the men who were building the dam—a boy perhaps fifteen, lithe and quick and dark, sharply handsome. When he saw me, he made all his actions more exaggerated—his strides were longer, and when he carried an axe over to a man who yelled for it, he swaggered.

That was the first time I ever didn't hate being a girl—when I saw that nice boy and saw that he noticed I was there and put on an act for me. I wonder what ever became of that half-breed boy.

Maybe, I thought, *Steve Morris is building that dam just to show off to Mary.* I know now, of course, that the dam was tremendously more important to him than Mary was, and that he was more important to Mary than anything else in the world; more important, even, than her hope of ceasing to be a tepee Indian.

It was only a few minutes that I watched the half-breed boy. Mary had to call me twice before I heard her. We had forgotten to eat our picnic lunch, but we gobbled it just before we reached the ranch.

When we were saying good-bye, she did a thing unusual for her —she put her arm around my waist as we walked toward the house. 'Could you keep a secret?' she asked.

'Sure. Sure I could. What is it?'

'Steve is going to test the dam tomorrow,' she whispered. 'And next time I see you, maybe I'll tell you another secret.'

That night my mother said we simply had to go home I kicked up a fuss that must have broken a record, but Ma was firm.

'I've got work to do,' she said flatly. 'I can't leave your poor father there alone forever.'

'Then let the child stay with us for a few days,' Mrs Riley begged. My, she was a kind, understanding woman. 'I haven't any girls of my own. I'd be glad to have a little girl around. One of the boys can ride back with her next week.'

I had sense enough to be quiet while they argued it out, and Mrs Riley won.

The day wore on, and Mary didn't come. I found I didn't like the Rileys' place so well, after all, because I had to be a good girl and not have tantrums. Ma had been pretty outspoken about that.

I was sitting by the window in the parlour, looking at an album full of pictures of people I didn't know, when I glanced out the window and saw brush bending towards me in the canyon. Then I saw water, and I called out proudly 'He's let the water on the dam, Miz Riley! Come look at the water!'

There was a hoarse shout from outside. Mr Riley thundered in. 'Up the hill! Run up the hill! There's water coming down the canyon!'

Mrs Riley grabbed me by the hand, and we ran without looking back.

Mr Riley and some other men wrestled with the stock before following us, and then there was no need for them to climb the hill at all, because it was plain that the water would not come even so high as the house.

It could not have been for more than fifteen minutes that the tumbling stream poured down the canyon and spread out where the main highway runs now, bringing with it pieces of lumber and branches and logs. It was not a big flood.

Immediately I wanted to go closer and see it. 'Come on!' I called.

Before anyone could tell me not to go, I ran down to the new spreading pond below the house. There was a man lying there, face down in the dirty water with his legs up on the water-flattened grass. I squeaked and turned to run back and then I saw another man with a brown shirt on. He was lying face up, with his eyes open and a log across his chest. I stumbled back up to the house, screaming.

So I didn't stay at the Rileys' after all. They sent me back that night. One of the Riley boys saddled a pony for me and one for himself, and we started right away. Mrs Riley's voice was shaking, and so were her hands, as she put my clothes into a bundle to tie on the saddle.

'Go fast, Mike,' she pleaded. 'Ride fast until you get her home. If her mother should hear of this before Beulah gets home, it would kill her.'

We rode all night through the quiet, windless hills. Sometimes I went ahead and sometimes Mike did. It was pretty dark and frightening, though Mike was packing a gun, just in case. After the first excitement died down and I was plain tired and sleepy, I hated that hard night ride, although it was something I had always dreamed of doing. I was nearer grown up after that night, more inclined to concern myself with the real present than with the impossible dream.

They found ten other men after the flood water had gone away. Just one man who had been down in the canyon when the dam broke had not drowned—the man who built the dam, Steve Morris. The boy I had liked had been on high ground with the rest of the crew.

Ma worried about me for a long time; I used to wake up crying and trembling. In the fall she decided to use psychology, though she had probably never heard of it. It was the kind of psychology they use on aviators now, when they make a man go up again right after he has had a crash. I wasn't afraid to go back to the place; I was eager for any change.

'Will Mary be there?' I demanded. 'Make her be there.'

'I suppose it could be arranged,' Ma said. 'I'll tell her folks.'

Mary was not at the ranch on the day we got there, but Mrs Riley said she would come. Ma asked a few questions about the valley when she thought I was outside.

'Steve had got several families to settle there,' Mrs Riley said. 'But they've got no water to run into their ditches, so they'll starve out. Everything's dried up. The valley was never meant to be settled, I guess.'

'Not good land?'

'Oh, yes. It's very fertile, Bob says, but people say it's unlucky.'

'That man who built the dam—where did he go?'

'Still there, I guess. My, he took it hard! Every nickel he had he gave to the families of those men who were killed, to help them get a new start. Did I tell you his hair turned grey? Bob was saying yesterday he hadn't seen him for weeks. Said he couldn't talk about anything except what he'd done that was wrong. He has a queer sort of conscience that eats on him. Seems to think this was a terrible punishment that fell on those others for his own sins.'

Ma must have been watching to see how I reacted to being back there, but it really didn't bother me. Except for grass that was matted where the water had been, you wouldn't have known there had been a flood. It was important to me, somehow, to see that the water was gone.

Ma and Mrs Riley pampered me considerably, and when I asked whether Mary and I could go for a long ride Ma said it was all right, and even packed us a lunch.

When Mary and her sullen brother rode down over the hill, I ran to meet them. Mary was thin, and she acted fidgety.

'We can take a lunch and go riding all afternoon!' I crowed.

'Did your mother say so?' she asked sharply.

'You bet she did,' I boasted, as if I'd horsewhipped her into it. Mary turned to her brother without even dismounting and spoke long and forcefully to him in their own language. He argued back, and I heard him groan 'No!' in English.

'Yes, you will,' she snapped. 'Do just as I said.'

He argued some more, but when he rode off he acted as if he meant to obey.

'We'll meet him later,' she told me. 'Don't tell anybody.'

She was in such a hurry that I didn't get the saddle cinched up tight enough. That cayuse was wise, and he'd blow himself up like a barrel so the cinch would loosen later. I almost fell off when the saddle turned, after we'd gone over a couple of hills. Mary was sharp and impatient with me while I fixed the cinch and gave the pony a warning punch with my knee.

We rode south and then turned west, down among cedars into darkness that was chilly because fall was coming. I recognized the canyon. This, I realized, was the place where all those men had gone tumbling with the water. I shivered and wished Mary had chosen some other place for us to ride.

'Wait,' she commanded suddenly. She called some words I could not understand. There was no answer. Farther on she called again, and a burly man came out of the woods into the trail, leading a horse. I was startled until I saw it was only her brother.

I said hello civilly, and he grunted some question to Mary. After a little argument he got on his horse, and we all rode up the canyon. Nobody talked. We went clear to the end of the canyon, up the steep part that winds to High Valley. I saw the valley for the second time, spreading flat and golden-dry to high hills. It was sere and blasted.

'Wait here,' Mary said. We let our horses stand while her brother strolled over a rise and returned, shaking his head. I was wise enough to know that he was unwillingly helping Mary to look for Steve Morris, who should have been in one of the shacks there.

On the way back down the canyon Mary rode in front, with her shawl over her bowed head. She stopped her horse so abruptly that mine bumped him. She slid out of the saddle and almost fell. She pointed at something on the ground that I could not even see and spoke rapidly to her brother. He dismounted and looked at the ground sharply. Grumbling, he got back on his horse and shouldered through brush down towards the now docile creek that talked to itself over its stones.

He shouted something from below, and Mary plunged her horse recklessly through the brush. Not knowing what else to do, I followed.

I cried out, because there was a man lying on the grassy flat, and I had dreamed of men lying in the water. This one was not in the water. He was lying on a blanket by the creek, and he was not dead, but he looked near it. His face was so gaunt that it was shiny, and his hair and beard were shot with grey, but he had a look of youngness about him.

'Steve!' Mary whispered. 'Steve! Are you hurt?'

'No,' he said and closed his eyes.

She looked about, and my eyes followed hers. The grass was trampled flat; he had been camping there for a long time, but there was no sign of food or of a fire. There was a can that he had used for drinking from the creek, but he had no frying pan. He had only the rusted can and the blanket he lay on, waiting.

Mary stood over him. 'Get up, Steve. We'll take you back to the valley.'

'I can't go back,' he said. 'Those men—'

She misunderstood him. 'Those men are dead. They can't hurt you.'

'They're dead,' he said. 'My fault.'

There was a long silence as she thought with his thoughts until she understood him.

'You won't help by lying here starving to death,' she said shortly.

He smiled a little and his teeth showed.

'How long have you been here without eating?' she asked.

'Eleven days,' he whispered.

Mary turned her back and covered her face with her shawl. Then she faced him again in desperation.

'You didn't kill those men. The water did it.'

'I let the water in.'

'No, you didn't. The dam broke.'

'I built the dam.'

'You can't help them now!' she insisted.

'A life for a life,' he said slowly. 'I have only one. There were ... twelve.' He looked earnestly up into her face, not moving. 'Mary, don't you understand? I wanted something I ... should not have.'

She bowed her head and answered in a muffled voice, 'I didn't know ... white men believed in sacrifices this way.'

Then there was forest silence, rippled only by the incoherent speech of the creek talking dangerously to itself under the cedars.

Mary looked at Steve again. 'I know a way to make sacrifice,' she said softly. 'I know a better way than yours.'

Steve did not answer, but he watched her face.

'The way of my people,' Mary said. 'I can make medicine to quiet the spirits of the dead. To pay your debt because you wanted something you should not have.'

I was astonished, because I knew that Indian women of Mary's tribe couldn't make medicine. Mary's brother stared at her.

She snapped at her brother, argued with him, flung out her arm in a commanding gesture, repeating some phrase over and over. He grunted, but he went away and then came back, bringing bark and twigs for a fire. She took them from his hands.

'This is big medicine,' she said softly. 'I can make this medicine. Nobody else can do it. It is sacrifice.'

She stooped and set the twigs and bark for a tiny, peaked fire. She moved her hands over it and murmured. She turned her face to the sky and spoke softly. Then she took a match from her brother's hand and lighted the fire. She knelt by it, swaying and whispering, moving her hands in the thin stream of smoke. I heard the cedars clicking around where I sat, transfixed with fright, on my pony. The smoke went straight up without a quiver. It was not wind that moved the cedars.

Mary took water from the creek into the rusted can and heated it, speaking softly all the while. She opened our picnic lunch and took out a piece of bread. Holding it high in her hands, she spoke to the sky. Then she broke the bread into the hot water in the can.

She spoke to her brother in their own tongue, and he lifted up Steve Morris. Stooping, she kissed Steve Morris on the forehead. Then she held the can to his lips.

'This is magic,' she told him. 'Take it.... No, don't touch my hands. I can't touch you again. Never again. Take it. Drink it.'

Too weak to resist, Steve Morris took the bread-and-water mixture into his mouth and swallowed. When he had finished it, Mary's brother laid him down again.

Mary stood with the fire between her and Steve Morris; she stood wrapped in her shawl.

'That is big medicine,' she said in the guttural voice of an Indian woman. 'But you have to pay back for medicine. I have made an offering for you. I will never speak to you again, and if you ever see me, you will not know. You will have strength now that you did not have before. Steve Morris, go back to the valley!' She bowed her shoulders under the shawl. 'Indian woman go back to her people,' she said.

If she had seen me, she might have been horrified, as I was, to know that I was there, but she was blind with tears. I rode down the trail behind her after her brother had bundled Steve onto his own pony and had taken him back up the canyon.

I honestly do not believe that she performed any Indian ceremony over that fire. Probably she did not even know any. But she knew what a man needed when he was starving himself to death. He needed to be fed, but he also needed a compulsion put upon him to make him go on fighting. She laid on him such a burden that he did not dare to die. And she took on herself the burden of never seeing him again, so that he would always remember.

They rode in the same bright procession, on the day forty-odd years later when the settlers of High Valley celebrated the road they finally got, years after the Government built them a dam. But Steve Morris could not have known who Mary Waters was, so truly had she done what she had promised. And you would not have known, when he rode wearily in his triumphal procession, that once Steve Morris had been a weak-souled man and a quitter.

It was not Indian magic that Mary Waters made; it was woman magic. But only a great woman could have made that sacrifice.

A few days after school started I stopped Joe Hawk when he was going out of my English class. 'Next time you see your grandmother,' I said to him, 'ask her if she remembers me. I think she used to be a friend of mine.'

'Aw, she couldn't be the one,' he scoffed. 'She wears a blanket. She don't even talk English.'

The Gift of Cochise

Tense, and white to the lips, Angie Lowe stood in the door of her cabin with a double-barrelled shotgun in her hands. Beside the door was a Winchester '73, and on the table inside the house were two Walker Colts.

Facing the cabin were twelve Apaches on ragged calico ponies, and one of the Indians had lifted his hand, palm outwards. The Apache sitting on the white-splashed bay pony was Cochise.

Beside Angie were her seven-year-old son Jimmy and her five-year-old daughter Jane.

Cochise sat on his pony in silence; his black, unreadable eyes studied the woman, the children, the cabin, and the small garden. He looked at the two ponies in the corral and the three cows. His eyes strayed to the small stack of hay cut from the meadow, and to the few steers farther up the canyon.

Three times the warriors of Cochise had attacked this solitary cabin and three times they had been turned back. In all, they had lost seven men, and three had been wounded. Four ponies had been killed. His braves reported that there was no man in the house, only a woman and two children, so Cochise had come to see for himself this woman who was so certain a shot with a rifle and who killed his fighting men.

These were some of the same fighting men who had outfought, outguessed and outrun the finest American army on record, an army outnumbering the Apaches by a hundred to one. Yet a lone woman with two small children had fought them off, and the woman was scarcely more than a girl. And she was prepared to fight now. There was a glint of admiration in the old eyes that appraised her. The Apache was a fighting man, and he respected fighting blood.

'Where is your man?'

'He had gone to El Paso.' Angie's voice was steady, but she was frightened as she had never been before. She recognized Cochise from descriptions, and she knew that if he decided to kill or capture her it would be done. Until now, the sporadic attacks

she had fought off had been those of casual bands of warriors
who raided her in passing.

'He has been gone a long time. How long?'

Angie hesitated, but it was not in her to lie. 'He has been gone
four months.'

Cochise considered that. No one but a fool would leave such a
woman, or such fine children. Only one thing could have pre-
vented his return. 'Your man is dead,' he said.

Angie waited, her heart pounding with heavy, measured beats.
She had guessed long ago that Ed had been killed but the way
Cochise spoke did not imply that Apaches had killed him, only
that he must be dead or he would have returned.

'You fight well,' Cochise said. 'You have killed my young
men.'

'Your young men attacked me.' She hesitated, then added,
'They stole my horses.'

'Your man is gone. Why do you not leave?'

'Angie looked at him with surprise. 'Leave? Why, this is my
home. This land is mine. This spring is mine. I shall not leave.'

'This was an Apache spring,' Cochise reminded her reasonably.

'The Apache lives in the mountains,' Angie replied. 'He does
not need this spring. I have two children, and I do need it.'

'But when the Apache comes this way, where shall he drink?
His throat is dry and you keep him from water.'

The very fact that Cochise was willing to talk raised her hopes.
There had been a time when the Apache made no war on the
white man. 'Cochise speaks with a forked tongue,' she said. 'There
is water yonder.' She gestured towards the hills, where Ed had
told her there were springs. 'But if the people of Cochise come in
peace they may drink at this spring.'

The Apache leader smiled faintly. Such a woman would rear
a nation of warriors. He nodded at Jimmy. 'The small one—does
he also shoot?'

'He does,' Angie said proudly, 'And well, too!' She pointed to
an upthrust leaf of prickly pear. 'Show them, Jimmy.'

The prickly pear was an easy two hundred yards away, and the
Winchester was long and heavy, but he lifted it eagerly and
steadied it against the doorjamb as his father had taught him, held
his sight an instant, then fired. The bud on top of the prickly
pear disintegrated.

There were grunts of appreciation from the dark-faced warriors.
Cochise chuckled. 'The little warrior shoots well. It is well you

have no man. You might raise an army of little warriors to fight my people.'

'I have no wish to fight your people,' Angie said quietly. 'Your people have your ways, and I have mine. I live in peace when I am left in peace. I did not think,' she added with dignity, 'that the great Cochise made war on women!'

The Apache looked at her, then turned his pony away. 'My people will trouble you no longer.' he said. 'You are the mother of a strong son.'

'What about my two ponies?' she called after him. 'Your young men took them from me.'

Cochise did not turn or look back, and the little cavalcade of riders followed him away. Angie stepped back into the cabin and closed the door. Then she sat down abruptly, her face white, the muscles in her legs trembling.

When morning came, she went cautiously to the spring for water. Her ponies were back in the corral. They had been returned during the night.

Slowly, the days drew on. Angie broke a small piece of the meadow and planted it. Alone, she cut hay in the meadow and built another stack. She saw Indians several times, but they did not bother her. One morning, when she opened her door, a quarter of antelope lay on the step, but no Indian was in sight. Several times, during the weeks that followed, she saw moccasin tracks near the spring.

Once, going out at daybreak, she saw an Indian girl dipping water from the spring. Angie called to her, and the girl turned quickly, facing her. Angie walked toward her, offering a bright red silk ribbon. Pleased, the Apache girl left.

And the following morning there was another quarter of antelope on her step—but she saw no Indian.

Ed Lowe had built the cabin in West Dog Canyon in the spring of 1871, but it was Angie who chose the spot, not Ed. In Santa Fe they would have told you that Ed Lowe was good-looking, shiftless and agreeable. He was also unfortunately handy with a pistol.

Angie's father had come from County Mayo to New York and from New York to the Mississippi, where he became a tough, brawling river boatman. In New Orleans, he met a beautiful Cajun girl and married her. Together, they started west for Santa Fe, and Angie was born en route. Both parents died of cholera when Angie was fourteen. She lived with an Irish family for the following three years, then married Ed Lowe when she was seventeen.

Santa Fe was not good for Ed, and Angie kept after him until they started south. It was Apache country, but they kept on until they reached the old Spanish ruin in West Dog. Here there were grass, water, and shelter from the wind.

There was fuel, and there were piñons and game. And Angie, with an Irish eye for the land, saw that it would grow crops.

The house itself was built on the ruins of the old Spanish building, using the thick walls and the floor. The location had been admirably chosen for defence. The house was built in a corner of the cliff, under the sheltering overhang, so that approach was possible from only two directions, both covered by an easy field of fire from the door and windows.

For seven months, Ed worked hard and steadily. He put in the first crop, he built the house, and proved himself a handy man with tools. He repaired the old plough they had bought, cleaned out the spring, and paved and walled it with slabs of stone. If he was lonely for the carefree companions of Santa Fe, he gave no indication of it. Provisions were low, and when he finally started off to the south, Angie watched him go with an ache in her heart.

She did not know whether she loved Ed. The first flush of enthusiasm had passed, and Ed Lowe had proved something less than she had believed. But he had tried, she admitted. And it had not been easy for him. He was an amiable soul, giving to whittling and idle talk, all of which he missed in the loneliness of the Apache country. And when he rode away, she had no idea whether she would ever see him again. She never did.

Santa Fe was far away to the north, but the growing village of El Passo was less than a hundred miles to the west, and it was there Ed Lowe rode for supplies and seed.

He had several drinks—his first in months—in one of the saloons. As the liquor warmed his stomach, Ed Lowe looked around agreeably. For a moment, his eyes clouded with worry as he thought of his wife and children back in Apache country, but it was not in Ed Lowe to worry for long. He had another drink and leaned on the bar, talking to the bartender. All Ed had ever asked of life was enough to eat, a horse to ride, an occasional drink, and companions to talk with. Not that he had anything important to say. He just liked to talk.

Suddenly a chair grated on the floor, and Ed turned. A lean, powerful man with a shock of uncut black hair and torn, weather-faded shirt stood at bay. Facing him across the table were three hard-faced young men, obviously brothers.

Ches Lane did not notice Ed Lowe watching from the bar. He had eyes only for the men facing him. 'You done that deliberate!' The statement was a challenge.

The broad-chested man on the left grinned through broken teeth. 'That's right, Ches. I done it deliberate. You killed Dan Tolliver on the Brazos.'

'He made the quarrel.' Comprehension came to Ches. He was boxed, and by three of the fighting, blood-hungry Tollivers.

'Don't make no difference,' the broad-chested Tolliver said. '"Who sheds a Tolliver's blood, by a Tolliver's hand must die!"'

Ed Lowe moved suddenly from the bar. 'Three to one is long odds,' he said, his voice low and friendly. 'If the gent in the corner is willin', I'll side him.'

Two Tollivers turned towards him. Ed Lowe was smiling easily, his hand hovering near his gun. 'You stay out of this!' one of the brothers said harshly.

'I'm in,' Ed replied. 'Why don't you boys light a shuck?'

'No, by—!' The man's hand dropped for his gun, and the room thundered with sound.

Ed was smiling easily, unworried as always. His gun flashed up. He felt it leap in his hand, saw the nearest Tolliver smashed back, and he shot him again as he dropped. He had only time to see Ches Lane with two guns out and another Tolliver down when something struck him through the stomach and he stepped back against the bar, suddenly sick.

The sound stopped, and the room was quiet, and there was the acrid smell of powder smoke. Three Tollivers were down and dead, and Ed Lowe was dying. Ches Lane crossed to him.

'We got 'em,' Ed said. 'We sure did. But they got me.'

Suddenly his face changed. 'Oh, Lord in heaven, what'll Angie do?' And then he crumpled over on the floor and lay still, the blood staining his shirt and mingling with the sawdust.

Stiff-faced, Ches looked up. 'Who was Angie?' he asked.

'His wife,' the bartender told him. 'She's up northeast some-where, in Apache country. He was tellin' me about her. Two kids, too.'

Ches Lane stared down at the crumpled, used-up body of Ed Lowe. The man had saved his life.

One he could have beaten, two he might have beaten; three

would have killed him. Ed Lowe, stepping in when he did, had saved the life of Ches Lane.

'He didn't say where?'

'No.'

Ches Lane shoved his hat back on his head. 'What's northeast of here?'

The bartender rested his hands on the bar. 'Cochise,' he said. . . .

For more than three months, whenever he could rustle the grub, Ches Lane quartered the country over and back. The trouble was, he had no lead to the location of Ed Lowe's homestead. An examination of Ed's horse revealed nothing. Lowe had bought seed and ammunition, and the seed indicated a good water supply, and the ammunition implied trouble. But in that country there was always trouble.

A man had died to save his life, and Ches Lane had a deep sense of obligation. Somewhere that wife waited, if she was still alive, and it was up to him to find her and look out for her. He rode northeast, cutting for sign, but found none. Sandstorms had wiped out any hope of back-trailing Lowe. Actually, West Dog Canyon was more east than north, but this he had no way of knowing.

North he went, skirting the rugged San Andreas Mountains. Heat baked him hot, dry winds parched his skin. His hair grew dry and stiff and alkali-whitened. He rode north, and soon the Apaches knew of him. He fought them at a lonely water hole, and he fought them on the run. They killed his horse, and he switched his saddle to the spare and rode on. They cornered him in the rocks, and he killed two of them and escaped by night.

They trailed him through the White Sands, and he left two more for dead. He fought fiercely and bitterly, and would not be turned from his quest. He turned east through the lava beds and still more east to the Pecos. He saw only two white men, and neither knew of a white woman.

The bearded man laughed harshly. 'A woman alone? She wouldn't last a month! By now the Apaches got her, or she's dead. Don't be a fool! Leave this country before you die here.'

Lean, wind-whipped and savage, Ches Lane pushed on. The Mescaleros cornered him in Rawhide Draw and he fought them to a standstill. Grimly, the Apaches clung to his trail.

The sheer determination of the man fascinated them. Bred and born in a rugged and lonely land, the Apaches knew the difficulties of survival; they knew how a man could live, how he must live. Even as they tried to kill this man, they loved him, for he was one of their own.

Lane's jeans grew ragged. Two bullet holes were added to the old black hat. The slicker was torn; the saddle, so carefully kept until now, was scratched by gravel and brush. At night he cleaned his guns and by day he scouted the trails. Three times he found lonely ranch houses burned to the ground, the buzzard- and coyote-stripped bones of their owners lying nearby.

Once he found a covered wagon, its canvas flapping in the wind, a man lying sprawled on the seat with a pistol near his hand. He was dead and his wife was dead, and their canteens rattled like empty skulls.

Leaner every day, Ches Lane pushed on. He camped one night in a canyon near some white oaks. He heard a hoof click on stone and he backed away from his tiny fire, gun in hand.

The riders were white men, and there were two of them. Joe Tompkins and Wiley Lynn were headed west, and Ches Lane could have guessed why. They were men he had known before, and he told them what he was doing.

Lynn chuckled. He was a thin-faced man with lank yellow hair and dirty fingers. 'Seems a mighty strange way to get a woman. There's some as comes easier.'

'This ain't for fun,' Ches replied shortly. 'I got to find her.'

Tompkins stared at him. 'Ches, you're crazy! That gent declared himself in of his own wish and desire. Far's that goes, the gal's dead. No woman could last this long in Apache country.'

At daylight, the two men headed west, and Ches Lane turned south.

Antelope and deer are curious creatures, often led to their death by curiosity. The long-horn, soon going wild on the plains, acquires the same characteristic. He is essentially curious. Any new thing or strange action will bring his head up and his ears alert. Often a longhorn, like a deer, can be lured within a stone's throw by some queer antic, by a handkerchief waving, by a man under a hide, by a man on foot.

This character of the wild things holds true of the Indian. The lonely rider who fought so desperately and knew the desert so well soon became a subject of gossip among the Apaches. Over the fires of many a rancheria they discussed this strange rider who seemed to be going nowhere, but always riding, like a lean wolf dog on a trail. He rode across the mesas and down the canyons; he studied sign at every water hole; he looked long from every ridge. It was obvious to the Indians that he searched for something—but what?

Cochise had come again to the cabin in West Dog Canyon. 'Little warrior too small,' he said, 'too small for hunt. You join my people. Take Apache for man.'

'No.' Angie shook her head. 'Apache ways are good for the Apache, and the white man's ways are good for white men—and women.'

They rode away and said no more, but that night, as she had on many other nights after the children were asleep, Angie cried. She wept silently, her head pillowed on her arms. She was as pretty as ever, but her face was thin, showing the worry and struggle of the months gone by, the weeks and months without hope.

The crops were small but good. Little Jimmy worked beside her. At night, Angie sat alone on the steps and watched the shadows gather down the long canyon, listening to the coyotes yepping from the rim of the Guadalupes, hearing the horses blowing in the corral. She watched, still hopeful, but now she knew that Cochise was right: Ed would not return.

But even if she had been ready to give up this, the first home she had known, there could be no escape. Here she was protected by Cochise. Other Apaches from other tribes would not so willingly grant her peace.

At daylight she was up. The morning air was bright and balmy, but soon it would be hot again. Jimmy went to the spring for water, and when breakfast was over, the children played while Angie sat in the shade of a huge old cottonwood and sewed. It was a Sunday, warm and lovely. From time to time, she lifted her eyes to look down the canyon, half-smiling at her own foolishness.

The hard-packed earth of the yard was swept clean of dust; the pans hanging on the kitchen wall were neat and shining. The children's hair had been clipped, and there was a small bouquet on the kitchen table.

After a while, Angie put aside her sewing and changed her dress. She did her hair carefully, and then, looking in her mirror, she reflected with sudden pain that she was pretty, and that she was only a girl.

Resolutely, she turned from the mirror and, taking up her Bible, went back to the seat under the cottonwood. The children left their playing and came to her, for this was a Sunday ritual, their only one. Opening the Bible, she read slowly, '... though I walk through the valley of the shadow of death, I will fear no evil; for Thou art with me; Thy rod and Thy staff, they comfort me. Thou preparest a table before me in the presence of mine enemies: Thou....

'Mommy.' Jimmy tugged at her sleeve. 'Look!'

Ches Lane had reached a narrow canyon by mid-afternoon and decided to make camp. There was small possibility he would find another such spot, and he was dead tired, his muscles sodden with fatigue. The canyon was one of those unexpected gashes in the cap rock that gave no indication of its presence until you came right on it. After some searching, Ches found a route to the bottom and made a camp under a wind-hollowed overhang. There was water, and there was a small patch of grass.

After his horse had a drink and a roll on the ground, it began cropping eagerly at the rich, green grass, and Ches built a smokeless fire of ancient driftwood in the canyon bottom. It was his first hot meal in days, and when he had finished he put out his fire, rolled a smoke, and leaned back contentedly.

Before darkness settled, he climbed to the rim and looked over the country. The sun had gone down, and the shadows were growing long. After a half hour of study, he decided there was no living thing within miles, except for the usual desert life. Returning to the bottom, he moved his horse to fresh grass, then rolled in his blanket. For the first time in a month, he slept without fear.

He woke up suddenly in the broad daylight. The horse was listening to something, his head up. Swiftly, Ches went to the horse and led it back under the overhang. Then he drew on his boots, rolled his blankets, and saddled the horse. Still he heard no sound.

Climbing the rim again, he studied the desert and found nothing. Returning to his horse, he mounted up and rode down the canyon toward the flatland beyond. Coming out of the canyon mouth, he rode right into the middle of a war party of more than twenty Apaches—invisible until suddenly they stood up behind rocks, their rifles levelled. And he didn't have a chance.

Swiftly, they bound his wrists to the saddle horn and tied his feet. Only then did he see the man who led the party. It was Cochise.

He was a lean, wiry Indian of past fifty, his black hair streaked with grey, his features strong and clean-cut. He stared at Lane, and there was nothing in his face to reveal what he might be thinking.

Several of the young warriors pushed forward, talking excitedly and waving their arms. Ches Lane understood none of it, but he sat straight in the saddle, his head up, waiting. Then Cochise spoke and the party turned, and, leading his horse, they rode away.

The miles grew long and the sun was hot. He was offered no water and he asked for none. The Indians ignored him. Once a young brave rode near and struck him viciously. Lane made no sound, gave no indication of pain. When they finally stopped, it was beside a huge anthill swarming with big red desert ants.

Roughly, they untied him and jerked him from his horse. He dug in his heels and shouted at them in Spanish: 'The Apaches are women! They tie me to the ants because they are afraid to fight me!'

An Indian struck him, and Ches glared at the man. If he must die, he would show them how it should be done. Yet he knew the unpredictable nature of the Indian, of his great respect for courage.

'Give me a knife, and I'll kill any of your warriors!'

They stared at him, and one powerfully built Apache angrily ordered them to get on with it. Cochise spoke, and the big warrior replied angrily.

Ches Lane nodded at the anthill. 'Is this the death for a fighting man? I have fought your strong men and beaten them. I have left no trail for them to follow, and for months I have lived among you, and now only by accident have you captured me. Give me a knife,' he added grimly, 'and I will fight him!' He indicated the big, black-faced Apache.

The warrior's cruel mouth hardened, and he struck Ches across the face.

The white man tasted blood and fury. 'Woman!' Ches said. 'Coyote! You are afraid!' Ches turned on Cochise, as the Indians stood irresolute. 'Free my hands and let me fight!' he demanded. 'If I win, let me go free.'

Cochise said something to the big Indian. Instantly, there was stillness. Then an Apache sprang forward and, with a slash of his knife, freed Lane's hands. Shaking loose the thongs, Ches Lane chafed his wrists to bring back the circulation. An Indian threw a knife at his feet. It was his own bowie knife.

Ches took off his riding boots. In sock feet, his knife gripped low in his hand, its cutting edge up, he looked at the big warrior.

'I promise you nothing,' Cochise said in Spanish, 'but an honorable death.'

The big warrior came at him on cat feet. Warily, Ches circled. He had not only to defeat this Apache but to escape. He permitted himself a side glance towards his horse. It stood alone. No Indian held it.

The Apache closed swiftly, thrusting wickedly with the knife. Ches, who had learned knife-fighting in the bayou country of Louisiana, turned his hip sharply, and the blade slid past him. He struck swiftly, but the Apache's forward movement deflected the blade, and it failed to penetrate. However, as it swept up between the Indian's body and arm, it cut a deep gash in the warrior's left armpit.

The Indian sprang again, like a clawing cat, streaming blood. Ches moved aside, but a backhand sweep nicked him, and he felt the sharp bite of the blade. Turning, he paused on the balls of his feet.

He had had no water in hours. His lips were cracked. Yet he sweated now, and the salt of it stung his eyes. He stared into the malevolent black eyes of the Apache, then moved to meet him. The Indian lunged, and Ches sidestepped like a boxer and spun on the ball of his foot.

The sudden sidestep threw the Indian past him, but Ches failed to drive the knife into the Apache's kidney when his foot rolled on a stone. The point left a thin red line across the Indian's back. The Indian was quick. Before Ches could recover his balance, he grasped the whiteman's knife wrist. Desperately, Ches grabbed for the Indian's knife hand and got the wrist, and they stood there straining, chest to chest.

Seeing his chance, Ches suddenly let his knees buckle, then brought up his knee and fell back, throwing the Apache over his head to the sand. Instantly, he whirled and was on his feet, standing over the Apache. The warrior had lost his knife, and he lay there, staring up, his eyes black with hatred.

Coolly, Ches stepped back, picked up the Indian's knife, and tossed it to him contemptuously. There was a grunt from the watching Indians, and then his antagonist rushed. But the loss of blood had weakened the warrior, and Ches stepped in swiftly, struck the blade aside, then thrust the point of his blade hard against the Indian's belly.

Black eyes glared into his without yielding. A thrust, and the man would be disembowelled, but Ches stepped back. 'He is a strong man,' Ches said in Spanish. 'It is enough that I have won.'

Deliberately, he walked to his horse and swung into the saddle. He looked around, and every rifle covered him.

So he had gained nothing. He had hoped that mercy might lead to mercy, that the Apache's respect for a fighting man would win his freedom. He had failed. Again they bound him to his horse, but they did not take his knife from him.

When they camped at last, he was given food and drink. He was bound again, and a blanket was thrown over him. At daylight they were again in the saddle. In Spanish he asked where they were taking him, but they gave no indication of hearing. When they stopped again, it was beside a pole corral, near a stone cabin.

When Jimmy spoke, Angie got quickly to her feet. She recognized Cochise with a start of relief, but she saw instantly that this was a war party. And then she saw the prisoner.

Their eyes met and she felt a distinct shock. He was a white man, a big, unshaven man who badly needed both a bath and a haircut, his clothes ragged and bloody. Cochise gestured at the prisoner.

'No take Apache man, you take white man. This man good for hunt, good for fight. He strong warrior. You take 'em.'

Flushed and startled, Angie stared at the prisoner and caught a faint glint of humour in his dark eyes.

'Is this here the fate worse than death I hear tell of?' he inquired gently.

'Who are you?' she asked, and was immediately conscious that it was an extremely silly question.

The Apaches had drawn back and were watching curiously. She could do nothing for the present but accept the situation. Obviously they intended to do her a kindness, and it would not do to offend them. If they had not brought this man to her, he might have been killed.

'Name's Ches Lane, ma'am,' he said. 'Will you untie me? I'd feel a lot safer.'

'Of course.' Still flustered, she went to him and untied his hands. One Indian said something, and the others chuckled; then, with a whoop, they swung their horses and galloped off down the canyon.

Their departure left her suddenly helpless, the shadowy globe of her loneliness shattered by this utterly strange man standing before her, this big, bearded man brought to her out of the desert.

She smoothed her apron, suddenly pale as she realized what his delivery to her implied. What must he think of her? She turned away quickly. 'There's hot water,' she said hastily, to prevent his speaking. 'Dinner is almost ready.'

She walked quickly into the house and stopped before the stove, her mind a blank. She looked around her as if she had suddenly woken up in a strange place. She heard water being poured into the basin by the door, and heard him take Ed's razor. She had never moved the box. To have moved it would—

'Sight of work done here, ma'am.'

She hesitated, then turned with determination and stepped into the doorway. 'Yes, Ed.'

'You're Angie Lowe.'

Surprised, she turned toward him, and recognized his own startled awareness of her. As he shaved, he told her about Ed, and what had happened that day in the saloon.

'He—Ed was like that. He never considered consequences until it was too late.'

'Lucky for me he didn't.'

He was younger looking with his beard gone. There was a certain quiet dignity in his face. She went back inside and began putting plates on the table. She was conscious that he had moved to the door and was watching her.

'You don't have to stay,' she said. 'You owe me nothing. Whatever Ed did, he did because he was that kind of person. You aren't responsible.'

He did not answer, and when she turned again to the stove, she glanced swiftly at him. He was looking across the valley.

There was a studied deference about him when he moved to a place at the table. The children stared, wide-eyed and silent; it had been so long since a man sat at this table.

Angie could not remember when she had felt like this. She was awkwardly conscious of her hands, which never seemed to be in the right place or doing the right things. She scarcely tasted her food, nor did the children.

Ches Lane had no such inhibitions. For the first time, he realized how hungry he was. After the half-cooked meat of lonely trailside fires, this was tender and flavoured. Hot biscuits, desert honey . . . Suddenly he looked up, embarrassed at his appetite.

'You were really hungry,' she said.

'Man can't fix much, out on the trail.'

Later, after he'd got his bedroll from his saddle and unrolled it on the hay in the barn, he walked back to the house and sat on the lowest step. The sun was gone, and they watched the cliffs stretch their red shadows across the valley. A quail called plaintively, a mellow sound of twilight.

'You needn't worry about Cochise,' she said. 'He'll soon be crossing into Mexico.'

'I wasn't thinking about Cochise.'

That left her with nothing to say, and she listened again to the quail and watched a lone bright star.

'A man could get to like it here,' he said quietly.

Trap of Gold

Wetherton had been three months out of Horsehead before he found his first colour. At first it was a few scattered grains taken from the base of an alluvial fan where millions of tons of sand and silt had washed down from a chain of rugged peaks; yet the gold was ragged under the magnifying glass.

Gold that has been carried any distance becomes worn and polished by the abrasive action of the accompanying rocks and sand, so this could not have been carried far. With caution born of harsh experience he seated himself and lighted his pipe, yet excitement was strong within him.

A contemplative man by nature, experience had taught him how a man may be deluded by hope, yet all his instincts told him the source of the gold was somewhere on the mountain above. It could have come down the wash that skirted the base of the mountain, but the ragged condition of the gold made that improbable.

The base of the fan was a half-mile across and hundreds of feet thick, built of silt and sand washed down by centuries of erosion among the higher peaks. The point of the wide V of the fan lay between two towering upthrusts of granite, but from where Wetherton sat he could see that the actual source of the fan lay much higher.

Wetherton made camp near a tiny spring west of the fan, then picketed his burros and began his climb. When he was well over 2000 feet higher he stopped, resting again, and while resting he dry-panned some of the silt. Surprisingly, there were more than a few grains of gold even in that first pan, so he continued his climb, and passed at last between the towering portals of the granite columns.

Above this natural gate were three smaller alluvial fans that joined at the gate to pour into the greater fan below. Dry-panning two of these brought no results, but the third, even by the relatively poor method of dry-panning, showed a dozen colours, all of good size.

The head of this fan lay in a gigantic crack in a granite upthrust that resembled a fantastic ruin. Pausing to catch his breath, his gaze wandered along the base of this upthrust, and right before him the crumbling granite was slashed with a vein of quartz that was laced with gold!

Struggling nearer through the loose sand, his heart pounding more from excitement than from altitude and exertion, he came to an abrupt stop. The band of quartz was six feet wide and that six feet was cobwebbed with gold.

It was unbelievable, but here it was.

Yet even in this moment of success, something about the beetling cliff stopped him from going forward. His innate caution took hold and he drew back to examine it at greater length. Wary of what he saw, he circled the batholith and then climbed to the ridge behind it from which he could look down upon the roof. What he saw from there left him dry-mouthed and jittery.

The granite upthrust was obviously a part of a much older range, one that had weathered and worn, suffered from shock and twisting until finally this tower of granite had been violently upthrust, leaving it standing, a shaky ruin among younger and sturdier peaks. In the process the rock had been shattered and riven by mighty forces until it had become a miner's horror. Wetherton stared, fascinated by the prospect. With enormous wealth here for the taking, every ounce must be taken at the risk of life.

One stick of powder might bring the whole crumbling mass down in a heap, and it loomed all of three hundred feet above its base in the fan. The roof of the batholith was riven with gigantic cracks, seamed with breaks like the wall of an ancient building that has remained standing after heavy bombing. Walking back to the base of the tower, Wetherton found he could actually break loose chunks of the quartz with his fingers.

The vein itself lay on the downhill side and at the very base. The outer wall of the upthrust was sharply tilted so that a man working at the vein would be cutting his way into the very foundations of the tower, and any single blow of the pick might bring the whole mass down upon him. Furthermore, if the rock did fall, the vein would be hopelessly buried under thousands of tons of rock and lost without the expenditure of much more capital than he could command. And at this moment Wetherton's total of money in hand amounted to slightly less than forty dollars.

Thirty yards from the face he seated himself upon the sand and filled his pipe once more. A man might take tons out of there without trouble, and yet it might collapse at the first blow. Yet he knew he had no choice. He needed money and it lay here before him. Even if he were at first successful there were two things he must avoid. The first was tolerance of danger that might bring carelessness; the second, that urge to go back for that 'little bit more' that could kill him.

It was well into the afternoon and he had not eaten, yet he was not hungry. He circled the batholith, studying it from every angle only to reach the conclusion that his first estimate had been correct. The only way to get at the gold was to go into the very shadow of the leaning wall and attack it at its base, digging it out by main strength. From where he stood it seemed ridiculous that a mere man with a pick could topple that mass of rock, yet he knew how delicate such a balance could be.

The tower was situated on what might be described as the military crest of the ridge, and the alluvial fan sloped steeply away from its lower side, steeper than a steep stairway. The top of the leaning wall overshadowed the top of the fan, and if it started to crumble and a man had warning, he might run to the north with a bare chance of escape. The soft sand in which he must run would be an impediment, but that could be alleviated by making a walk from flat rocks sunken into the sand.

It was dusk when he returned to his camp. Deliberately, he had not permitted himself to begin work, not by so much as a sample. He must be deliberate in all his actions, and never for a second should he forget the mass that towered above him. A split second of hesitation when the crash came—and he accepted it as inevitable —would mean burial under tons of crumbled rock.

The following morning he picketed his burros on a small meadow near the spring, cleaned in the spring itself and prepared a lunch. Then he removed his shirt, drew on a pair of gloves and walked to the face of the cliff. Yet even then he did not begin, knowing that upon this habit of care and deliberation might depend not only his success in the venture, but life itself. He gathered flat stones and began building his walk. 'When you start moving,' he told himself, 'you'll have to be fast.'

Finally, and with infinite care, he began tapping at the quartz, enlarging cracks with the pick, removing fragments, then prying loose whole chunks. He did not swing the pick, but used it as a lever. The quartz was rotten, and a man might obtain a considerable amount by this method of picking or even pulling with the hands. When he had a sack filled with the richest quartz he carried it over his path to a safe place beyond the shadow of the tower.

Returning, he tamped a few more flat rocks into his path, and began on the second sack. He worked with greater care than was, perhaps, essential. He was not and had never been a gambling man.

In the present operation he was taking a carefully calculated risk in which every eventuality had been weighed and judged. He needed the money and he intended to have it; he had a good idea of his chances of success, but knew that his gravest danger was to become too greedy, too much engrossed in his task.

Dragging the two sacks down the hill he found a flat block of stone and with a single jack proceeded to break up the quartz. It was a slow and a hard job but he had no better means of extracting the gold. After breaking or crushing the quartz much of the gold could be separated by a knife blade, for it was amazingly concentrated. With water from the spring Wetherton panned the remainder until it was too dark to see.

Out of his blankets by daybreak he ate breakfast and completed the extraction of the gold. At a rough estimate his first day's work would run to four hundred dollars. He made a cache for the gold sack and took the now empty ore sacks and climbed back to the tower.

The air was clear and fresh, the sun warm after the chill at night, and he liked the feel of the pick in his hands.

Laura and Tommy awaited him back in Horsehead, and if he was killed here, there was small chance they would ever know what had become of him. But he did not intend to be killed. The gold he was extracting from this rock was for them, and not for himself.

It would mean an easier life in a larger town, a home of their own and the things to make the home a woman desires, and it meant an education for Tommy. For himself, all he needed was the thought of that home to return to, his wife and son—and the desert itself. And one was as necessary to him as the other.

The desert would be the death of him. He had been told that many times, and did not need to be told, for few men knew the desert as he did. The desert was to him what an orchestra is to a fine conductor, what the human body is to a surgeon. It was his work, his life, and the thing he knew best. He always smiled when he looked first into the desert as he started a new trip. Would this be it?

The morning drew on and he continued to work with an even-paced swing of the pick, a careful filling of the sack. The gold showed bright and beautiful in the crystalline quartz which was so much more beautiful than the gold itself. From time to time as the morning drew on, he paused to rest and to breathe deeply of the fresh, clear air. Deliberately, he refused to hurry.

For nineteen days he worked tirelessly, eight hours a day at first, then lessening his hours to seven, and then to six. Wetherton did not explain to himself why he did this, but he realized it was becoming increasingly difficult to stay on the job. Again and again he would walk away from the rock face on one excuse or another, and each time he would begin to feel his scalp prickle, his steps grow quicker, and each time he returned more reluctantly.

Three times, beginning on the thirteenth, again on the seventeenth and finally on the nineteenth day, he heard movement within the tower. Whether that whispering in the rock was normal he did not know. Such a natural movement might have been going on for centuries. He only knew that it happened now, and each time it happened a cold chill went along his spine.

His work had cut a deep notch at the base of the tower, such a notch as a man might make in felling a tree, but wider and deeper. The sacks of gold, too, were increasing. They now numbered seven, and their total would, he believed, amount to more than five thousand dollars—probably nearer to six thousand. As he cut deeper into the rock the vein was growing richer.

He worked on his knees now. The vein had slanted downward as he cut into the base on the tower and he was all of nine feet into the rock with the great mass of it above him. If that rock gave way while he was working he would be crushed in an instant with no chance of escape. Nevertheless, he continued.

The change in the rock tower was not the only change, for he had lost weight and he no longer slept well. On the night of the twentieth day he decided he had six thousand dollars and his goal would be ten thousand. And the following day the rock was the richest ever! As if to tantalize him into working on and on, the deeper he cut the richer the ore became. By nightfall of that day he had taken out more than a thousand dollars.

Now the lust of the gold was getting into him, taking him by the throat. He was fascinated by the danger of the tower as well as the desire for the gold. Three more days to go—could he leave it then? He looked again at the tower and felt a peculiar sense of foreboding, a feeling that here he was to die, that he would never escape. Was it his imagination, or had the outer wall leaned a little more?

On the morning of the twenty-second day he climbed the fan

over a path that use had built into a series of continuous steps. He had never counted those steps but there must have been over a thousand of them. Dropping his canteen into a shaded hollow and pick in hand he started for the tower.

The forward tilt did seem somewhat more than before. Or was it the light? The crack that ran behind the outer wall seemed to have widened and when he examined it more closely he found a small pile of freshly run silt near the bottom of the crack. So it had moved!

Wetherton hesitated, staring at the rock with wary attention. He was a fool to go back in there again. Seven thousand dollars was more than he had ever had in his life before, yet in the next few hours he could take out at least a thousand dollars more and in the next three days he could easily have the ten thousand he had set for his goal.

He walked to the opening, dropped to his knees and crawled into the narrowing, flat-roofed hole. No sooner was he inside than fear climbed up into his throat. He felt trapped, stifled, but he fought down the mounting panic and began to work. His first blows were so frightened and feeble that nothing came loose. Yet, when he did get started, he began to work with a feverish intensity that was wholly unlike him.

When he slowed and then stopped to fill his sack he was gasping for breath, but despite his hurry the sack was not quite full. Reluctantly, he lifted his pick again, but before he could strike a blow, the gigantic mass above him seemed to creak like something tired and old. A deep shudder went through the colossal pile and then a deep grinding that turned him sick with horror. All his plans for instant flight were frozen and it was not until the groaning ceased that he realized he was lying on his back, breathless with fear and expectancy. Slowly, he edged his way into the air and walked, fighting the desire to run, away from the rock.

When he stopped near his canteen he was wringing with cold sweat and trembling in every muscle. He sat down on the rock and fought for control. It was not until some twenty minutes had passed that he could trust himself to get to his feet.

Despite his experience, he knew that if he did not go back now he would never go. He had out but one sack for the day and wanted another. Circling the batholith he examined the widening crack, endeavouring again, for the third time, to find another means of access to the vein.

The tilt of the outer wall was obvious, and it could stand no more without toppling. It was possible that by cutting into the wall of the column and striking down he might tap the vein at a safer point. Yet this added blow at the foundation would bring the tower nearer to collapse and render his other hole untenable. Even this new attempt would not be safe, although immeasurably more secure than the hole he had left. Hesitating, he looked back at the hole.

Once more? The ore was now fabulously rich, and the few pounds he needed to complete the sack he could get in just a little while. He stared at the black and undoubtedly narrower hole, then looked up at the leaning wall. He picked up his pick and, his mouth dry, started back, drawn by a fascination that was beyond all reason.

His heart pounding, he dropped to his knees at the tunnel face. The air seemed stifling and he could feel his scalp tingling, but once he started to crawl it was better. The face where he now worked was at least sixteen feet from the tunnel mouth. Pick in hand, he began to wedge chunks from their seat. The going seemed harder now and the chunks did not come loose so easily. Above him the tower made no sound. The crushing weight was now something tangible. He could almost feel it growing, increasing with every move of his. The mountain seemed resting on his shoulder, crushing the air from his lungs.

Suddenly he stopped. His sack almost full, he stopped and lay very still, staring up at the bulk of the rock above him.

No.

He would go no further. Now he would quit. Not another sackful. Not another pound. He would go out now. He would go down the mountain without a backward look, and he would keep going. His wife waiting at home, little Tommy, who would run gladly to meet him—these were too much to gamble.

With the decision came peace, came certainty. He sighed deeply, and relaxed, and then it seemed to him that every muscle in his body had been knotted with strain. He turned on his side and with great deliberation gathered his lantern, his sack, his hand-pick.

He had won. He had defeated the crumbling tower, he had defeated his own greed. He backed easily, without the caution that had marked his earlier movements in the cave. His blind, trusting foot found the projecting rock, a piece of quartz that stuck out from the rough-hewn wall.

The blow was too weak, too feeble to have brought forth the reaction that followed. The rock seemed to quiver like the flesh of a beast when stabbed; a queer vibration went through that ancient rock, then a deep, gasping sigh.

He had waited too long!

Fear came swiftly in upon him, crowding him, while his body twisted, contracting into the smallest possible space. He tried to will his muscles to move beneath the growing sounds that vibrated through the passage. The whispers of the rock grew into a terrifying groan, and there was a rattle of pebbles. Then silence.

The silence was more horrifying than the sound. Somehow he was crawling, even as he expected the avalanche of gold to bury him. Abruptly, his feet were in the open. He was out.

He ran without stopping, but behind him he heard a growing roar that he couldn't outrace. When he knew from the slope of the land that he must be safe from falling rock, he fell to his knees. He turned and looked back. The muted, roaring sound, like thunder beyond mountains, continued, but there was no visible change in the tower. Suddenly, as he watched, the whole rock formation seemed to shift and tip. The movement lasted only seconds, but before the tons of rock had found their new equilibrium, his tunnel and the area around it had utterly vanished from sight.

When he could finally stand Wetherton gathered up his sack of ore and his canteen. The wind was cool upon his face as he walked away; and he did not look back again.

Emmet Dutrow

Three days he was there on the rock ledge. I don't think he left it
once. I couldn't be sure. I had things to do. But I could see him
from my place and each time I looked he was there, a small dark-
clad figure, immeasurably small against the cliff wall rising behind
him.

Sometimes he was standing, head back and face up. Sometimes
he was kneeling, head down and sunk into his shoulders. Sometimes he was sitting on one of the smaller stones.

Three days it was. And maybe the nights too. He was there when
I went in at dusk and he was there when I came out in early
morning. Once or twice I thought of going to him. But that would
have accomplished nothing. I doubt whether he would even have
noticed me. He was lost in an aloneness no one could penetrate.
He was waiting for his God to get around to considering his case.

I guess this is another you'll have to let me tell in my own way.
And the only way I know to tell it is in pieces, the way I saw it.

Emmet Dutrow was his name. He was of Dutch blood, at least
predominantly so; the hard-shell deep-burning kind. He came from
Pennsylvania, all the way to our new State of Wyoming with his
heavy wide-bed wagon and slow, swinging yoke of oxen. He must
have been months on the road, making his twelve to twenty miles
a day when the weather was good and little or none when it was
bad. The wagon carried food and farm tools and a few sparse
pieces of stiff furniture beneath an old canvas. He walked and must
have walked the whole way close by the heads of his oxen, guid-
ing them with a leather thong fastened to the yoke. And behind
about ten paces and to the side came his woman and his son Jess.

They camped that first night across the creek from my place.
I saw him picketing the oxen for grazing and the son building a
fire and the woman getting her pans from where they hung under
the wagon's rear axle, and when my own chores were done and I
was ready to go in for supper, I went to the creek and across on the
stones in the shallows and towards their fire. He stepped out from

it to confront me, blocking my way forward. He was a big man, big and broad and bulky, made more so by the queer clothes he wore. They were plain black of some rough thick material, plain black loose-fitting pants and plain black jacket like a frock-coat without any tails, and a plain black hat, shallow-crowned and stiff-brimmed. He had a square trimmed beard that covered most of his face, hiding the features, and eyes sunk far back so that you felt like peering close to see what might be in them.

Behind him the other two kept by the fire, the woman shapeless in a dark linsey-woolsey dress and pulled-forward shielding bonnet, the son dressed like his father except that he wore no hat.

I stopped. I couldn't have gone farther without walking right into him.

''Evening, stranger,' I said.

'Good evening,' he said. His voice was deep and rumbled in his throat with the self-conscious roll some preachers have in the pulpit. 'Have you business with me?'

'There's a quarter of beef hanging in my springhouse,' I said. 'I thought maybe you'd appreciate some fresh meat.'

'And the price?' he said.

'No price,' I said. 'I'm offering you some.'

He stared at me. At least the shadow-holes where his eyes hid were aimed at me. 'I'll be bounden to no man,' he said.

The son had edged out from the fire to look at me. He waved an arm at my place across the creek. 'Say mister,' he said. 'Are those cattle of yours—'

'Jess!' The father's voice rolled at him like a whip uncoiling. The son flinched at the sound and stepped back by the fire. The father turned his head again to me. 'Have you any further business?'

'No,' I said. I swung about and went back across the creek on the stones and up the easy slope to my little frame ranchhouse.

The next day he pegged his claim, about a third of a mile farther up the valley where it narrowed and the spring floods of centuries ago had swept around the curve above and washed the rock formation bare, leaving a high cliff to mark where they had turned. His quarter section spanned the space from the cliff to the present-day creek. It was a fair choice on first appearances; good bottom land, well-watered with a tributary stream wandering through, and there was a stand of cottonwoods back by the cliff. I had passed it up because I knew how the drifts would pile in below the cliff in winter. I was snug in the bend in the valley and the hills behind protecting me. It was plain he didn't know this kind of country. He was right where the winds down the valley would hit him when the cold came dropping out of the mountains.

He was a hard worker and his son too. They were started on a cabin before the first morning was over, cutting and trimming logs and hauling them with the oxen. In two days they had the framework up and the walls shoulder high, and then the rain started and the wind, one of our late spring storms that carried a lingering chill and drenched everything open with a steady lashing beat. I thought of them there, up and across the creek, with no roof yet and unable to keep a fire going in such weather, and I pulled on boots and a slicker and an old hat and went out and waded across and went up to their place. It was nearly dark, but he and the son were still at work setting another log in place. They had taken pieces of the old canvas and cut holes for their heads and pulled the pieces down over their shoulders with their heads poking through. This made using their arms slow and awkward, but they were still working. He had run the wagon along one wall of the cabin, and with this covering one side and the rest of the old canvas fastened to hang down the other, it formed a low cavelike shelter. The woman was in there, sitting on branches for a floor, her head nearly bumping the bed of the wagon above. I could hear the inside drippings, different from the outside pattern, as the rain beat through the cracks of the wagon planks and the chinks of the log wall.

He stepped forward again to confront me and stop me, a big bulgy shape in his piece of canvas topped by the beard and hat with the shadow-holes in the eyes between.

'It's a little wet,' I said. 'I thought maybe you'd like to come over to my place where it's warm and dry till this storm wears itself out. I can rig enough bunks.'

'No,' he said, rolling his tone with the organ stops out. 'We shall do with what is ours.'

I started to turn away and I saw the woman peering out at me from her pathetic shelter, her face pinched and damp under the bonnet, and I turned back.

'Man alive,' I said, 'forget your pride or whatever's eating you and think of your wife and the boy.'

'I am thinking of them,' he said. 'And I am the shield that shall protect them.'

I swung about and started away, and when I had taken a few

steps his voice rolled after me. 'Perhaps you should be thanked, neighbour. Perhaps you mean well.'

'Yes,' I said, 'I did.'

I kept on going and I did not look back and I waded across the creek and went up to my house and in and turned the lamp up bright and tossed a couple more logs into the fireplace.

I tried once more, about two weeks later. He had his cabin finished then, roofed with bark slabs over close-set poles and the walls chinked tight with mud from the creek bottom. He had begun breaking ground. His oxen were handy for that. They could do what no team of horses could do, could lean to the yoke and dig their split hooves into the sod and pull a heavy ploughshare ripping through the roots of our tough buffalo grass.

That seemed to me foolish, tearing up sod that was perfect for good cattle, getting ready for dirt farming way out there far from any markets. But he was doing it right. With the ground ploughed deep and the sod turned over, the roots would be exposed and would rot all through the summer and fall and by the next spring the ground would be ready to be worked and planted. And meanwhile he could string his fences and build whatever sheds he would need and get his whole place in shape.

We ought to be getting really acquainted, I thought, being the only neighbours there in the valley and more than that, for the nearest other place was two miles away towards town. It was up to me to make the moves. I was the first in the valley. He was the second, the newcomer.

As I said, I tried once more. It was a Saturday afternoon and I was getting ready to ride to town and see if there was any mail and pick up a few things and rub elbows with other folks a bit and I thought of them there across the creek, always working and penned close with only a yoke of oxen that couldn't make the eight miles in less than half a day each way. I harnessed the team to the buckboard and drove bouncing across the creek and to their place. The woman appeared in the cabin doorway, shading her eyes and staring at me. The son stopped ploughing off to the right and let go of the plough handles and started towards me. The father came around the side of the cabin and waved him back and came close to my wagon and stopped and planted his feet firmly and looked at me.

'I'm heading towards town,' I said. 'I thought maybe you'd like a ride in the back. You can look the place over and meet some of the folks around here.'

'No, neighbour,' he said. He looked at me and then let his voice out a notch. 'Sin and temptation abide in towns. When we came past I saw the two saloons and a painted woman.'

'Hell, man,' I said, 'you find those things everywhere. They don't bite if you let them alone.'

'Ah, yes,' he said. 'Everywhere. All along the long way I saw them. They are everywhere. That is why I stopped moving at last. There is no escaping them in towns. Wherever people congregate, there is sin. I shall keep myself and mine apart.'

'All right,' I said. 'So you don't like people. But how about your wife and the boy? Maybe they'd like a change once in a while.'

His voice rolled out another notch. 'They are in my keeping.' He looked at me and the light was right and for the first time I saw his eyes, bright and hot in their shadow-holes. 'Neighbour,' he said, all stops out, 'have I trespassed on your property?'

I swung the team in an arc and drove back across the creek. I unharnessed the team and sent them out in the side pasture with slaps on their rumps. I whistled the grey in and saddled him and headed for town at a good clip.

That was the last time. After that I simply watched what was happening up the valley. You could sum up most of it with the one word—work. And the rest of it centred on the rock ledge at the base of the cliff where a hard layer jutted out about ten feet above the valley floor, flat on top like a big table. I saw him working there, swinging some tool, and after several days I saw what he was doing. He was cutting steps in the stone, chipping out steps to the ledge top. Then he took his son away from the ploughing for a day to help him heave and pry the fallen rocks off the ledge, all except three, a big squarish one and two smaller ones. Up against the big one he raised a cross made of two lengths of small log. Every day after that, if I was out early enough in the morning and late enough when the dusk was creeping in, I could see him and his woman and the son, all three of them on the ledge, kneeling, and I could imagine his voice rolling around them and echoing from the cliff behind them. And on Sundays, when there would be nothing else doing about their place at all, not even cooking-smoke rising from the cabin chimney, they would be there hours on end, the woman and the son sometimes sitting on the two smaller stones, and the father, from his position leaning over the big stone, apparently reading from a book spread open before him.

It was on a Sunday, in the afternoon, that the son trespassed on my place. He came towards the house slow and hesitating like he was afraid something might jump and snap at him. I was sitting on the porch, the Winchester across my knees, enjoying the sunshine and waiting to see if the gopher that had been making holes in my side pasture would show its head. I watched him come, a healthy young figure in his dark pants and homespun shirt. When he was close, I raised my voice.

'Whoa, Jess,' I said. 'Aren't you afraid some evil might scrape off me and maybe get on you?'

He grinned kind of foolish and scrubbed one shoe-toe in the dirt. 'Don't make fun of me,' he said. 'I don't hold with that stuff the way father does. He said I could come over anyway. He's decided perhaps you're all right.'

'Thanks,' I said. 'Since I've passed the test, why not step up here and sit a spell?'

He did, and he looked all around very curious and after a while he said: 'Father thought perhaps you could tell him what to do to complete the claim and get the papers on it.'

I told him, and we sat awhile, and then he said: 'What kind of a gun is that?'

'It's a Winchester,' I said. 'A repeater. A right handy weapon.'

'Could I hold it once?' he said.

I slipped on the safety and passed it to him. He set it to his shoulder and squinted along the barrel, awkward and self-conscious.

'Ever had a gun of your own?' I said.

'No,' he said. He handed the gun back quickly and stared at the porch floor. 'I never had anything of my own. Everything belongs to father. He hasn't a gun anyway. Only an old shotgun and he won't let me touch it.' And after a minute: 'I never had even a nickel of my own to buy a thing with.' And after a couple of minutes more: 'Why does he have to be praying all the time, can you tell me that? That's all he ever does, working and praying. Asking forgiveness for sins. For my sins and Ma's sins too. What kind of sins have we ever had a chance to do? Can you tell me that?'

'No,' I said. 'No, I can't.'

We sat awhile longer, and he was looking out at the pasture. 'Say, are those cattle—'

'Yes,' I said. 'They're Herefords. Purebreds. Some of the first in these parts. That's why they're fenced tight.'

'How'd you ever get them?' he said. 'I mean them and everything you've got here.'

'Well,' I said, 'I was a fool youngster blowing my money fast
as I found it. Then one day I decided I didn't like riding herd on
another man's cattle and bony longhorns at that when I knew there
were better breeds. So I started saving my pay.'

'How long did it take?' he said.

'It was eleven years last month,' I said, 'that I started a bank
account.'

'That's a long time,' he said. 'That's an awful long time.'

'How old are you, Jess?' I said.

'Nineteen,' he said. 'Nineteen four months back.'

'When you're older,' I said, 'it won't seem like such a long time.
When you're getting along some, time goes mighty fast.'

'But I'm not older,' he said.

'No.' I said. 'No. I guess you're not.'

We sat awhile longer and then I got foolish. 'Jess,' I said, 'the
ploughing's done. That was the big job. The pressure ought to be
letting up a bit now. Why don't you drop over here an afternoon
or two and help me with my haying. I'll pay fair wages. Twenty-
five cents an hour.'

His face lit like a match striking. 'Hey, mister!' Then: 'But
Father—'

'Jess,' I said, 'I never yet heard of work being sinful.'

I wondered whether he would make it and Wednesday he did,
coming early in the afternoon and sticking right with me till quitting hour. He was a good worker. He had to be to make up for the
time he wasted asking me questions about the country and people
roundabout, and my place and my stock and the years I'd spent
in the saddle. He was back again on Friday. When I called quits
and we went across the pasture to the house, the father was standing by the porch waiting.

'Good evening, neighbour,' he said. 'According to my son you
mentioned several afternoons. They are done. I have come for the
money.'

'Dutrow,' I said, 'Jess did the work. Jess gets the money.'

'You do not understand,' he said, the tone beginning to roll.
'My son is not yet of man's estate. Until he is I am responsible
for him and the fruit of his labour is mine. I am sworn to guard
him against evil. Money in an untried boy's pocket is a sore
temptation to sin.'

I went into the house and took three dollars from the purse in my jacket pocket and went out to Jess and put them in his hand. He stood there with the hand in front of him, staring down at it.

'Jess! Come here!'

He came, flinching and unwilling, the hand still stiff in front of him, and the father took the money from it.

'I'm sorry Jess,' I said. 'Looks like there's no point in your working here again.'

He swung his eyes at me the way a whipped colt does and turned and went away, trying to hold to a steady walk and yet stumbling forward in his hurry.

'Dutrow,' I said, 'I hope that money burns your hand. You have already sinned with it.'

'Neighbour,' he said, 'you take too much on yourself. My God alone shall judge my actions.'

I went into the house and closed the door.

It was about a month later, in the middle of the week, that the father himself came to see me, alone and in mid-morning and wearing his black coat and strange black hat under the hot sun as he came to find me.

'Neighbour,' he said, 'have you see my son this morning?'

'No,' I said.

'Strange,' he said. 'He was not on his pallet when I rose. He missed morning prayers completely. He has not appeared at all.'

He stood silent a moment. Then he raised an arm and pointed a thick forefinger at me. His voice rolled at its deepest. 'Neighbour,' he said, 'if you have contrived with my son to go forth into the world, I shall call down the wrath of my God upon you.'

'Neighbour Dutrow,' I said, 'I don't know what your son's doing. But I know what you're going to do. You're going to shut your yap and get the hell off my place.'

I don't think he heard me. He wiped a hand across his face and down over his beard. 'You must pardon me,' he said, 'I am sore overwrought with worry.'

He strode away, down to the creek and left along it out of the valley towards town. The coat flapped over his hips as he walked and he grew smaller in the distance till he rounded the first hill and disappeared.

He returned in late afternoon, still alone and dusty and tired, walking slowly and staring at the ground ahead of him. He went past on the other side of the creek and to his place and stopped at the door of the cabin and the woman emerged and they went to the rock ledge and they were still kneeling there when the dark shut them out of my sight.

The next day, well into the afternoon, I heard a horse coming along the trace that was the beginning of the road into the valley and Marshal Eakins rode up to me by the barn and swung down awkward and stiff. He was tired and worn and his left shoulder was bandaged with some of the cloth showing through the open shirt collar.

'Afternoon, John,' he said. 'Any coffee in the pot you could warm over?'

In the house I stirred the stove and put the pot on to heat. I pointed at his shoulder.

'One of our tough friends?' I said.

'Hell, no,' he said. 'I can handle them. This was an amateur. A crazy youngster.'

When he had his cup, he took a first sip and leaned back in his chair.

'That the Dutrow place up the creek?' he said.

'Yes,' I said.

'Must be nice neighbours,' he said. 'It was their boy drilled me.' He tried the cup again and finished it in four gulps and reached for the pot. 'His father was in town yesterday. Claimed the boy had run away. Right he was. The kid must have hid out during the day. Had himself a time at night. Pried a window at Walton's store. Packed himself a bag of food. Took a rifle and box of shells. Slipped over to the livery stable. Saddled a horse and lit out.'

'He couldn't ride,' I said.

'Reckon not,' Eakins said. 'Made a mess of the gear finding a bridle and getting it on. Left an easy track too. Didn't know how to make time on a horse. I took Patton and went after him. Must have had hours' start, but we were tailing him before ten. Got off or fell off, don't know which, and scrambled into some rocks. I told him we had the horse and if he'd throw out the gun and come out himself there wouldn't be too much fuss about it. But he went crazy wild. Shouted something about sin catching up with him and started blazing away.'

'He couldn't shoot,' I said.

'Maybe not,' Eakins said. 'But he was pumping the gun as fast as he could and he got Patton dead centre. We hadn't fired a shot.'

Eakins started on the second cup.

'Well?' I said.

'So I went in and yanked him out,' Eakins said. 'Reckon I was a little rough. Patton was a good man.'

He finished the second cup and set it down. 'Got to tell his folks. Thought maybe you'd go along. Women give me the fidgets.' He pushed at the cup with a finger. 'Not much time. The town's a little hot. Trial will be tomorrow.'

We walked down to the creek and across and up to their place. The woman appeared in the cabin doorway and stared at us. The father came from somewhere around the side of the cabin. He planted his feet firmly and confronted us. His head tilted high and his eyes were bright and hot in their shadow-holes. His voice rolled at us.

'You have found my son.'

'Yes,' Eakins said, 'we've found him.' He looked at me and back at the father and stiffened a little, and he told them, straight, factual. 'The trial will be at ten tomorrow,' he said. 'They'll have a lawyer for him. It's out of my hands. It's up to the judge now.'

And while he was talking, the father shrank right there before us. His head dropped and he seemed to dwindle inside his rough black clothes. His voice was scarcely more than a whisper.

'The sins of the fathers,' he said, and was silent.

It was the woman who was speaking, out from the doorway and stretching up tall and pointing at him, the first and only words I ever heard her speak.

'You did it,' she said. 'You put the thoughts of sin in his head, always praying about it. And keeping him cooped in with never a thing he could call his own. On your head it is in the eyes of God. You drove him to it.'

She stopped and stood still, looking at him, and her eyes were bright and hot and accusing in the pinched whiteness of her face, and she stood still, looking at him.

They had forgotten we were there. Eakins started to speak again and thought better of it. He turned to me and I nodded and we went back along the creek and across and to the barn and he climbed stiffly on his horse and started towards town.

In the morning I saddled the grey and rode to the Dutrows' place. I was thinking of offering him the loan of the team and the buckboard. There was no sign of any activity at all. The place looked deserted. The cabin door was open and I poked my head in. The woman was sitting on a straight chair by the dead fireplace. Her hands were folded in her lap and her head was bowed over them.

She was sitting still. There's no other way to describe what she was doing. She was just sitting.

'Where is he?' I said.

Her head moved in my direction and she looked vaguely at me and there was no expression on her face.

'Is he anywhere around?' I said.

Her head shook only enough for me to catch the slight movement and swung slowly back to its original position. I stepped back and took one more look around and mounted the grey and rode towards town, looking for him along the way, and did not see him.

I had no reason to hurry and when I reached the converted store building we used for a courthouse, it was fairly well crowded. Judge Cutler was on the bench. We had our own judge now for local cases. Cutler was a tall, spare man, full of experience and firm opinions, honest and independent in all his dealings with other people. That was why he was our judge. Marshall Eakins was acting as our sheriff until we would be better organized and have an office established. That was why he had taken charge the day before.

They brought in Jess Dutrow and put him in a chair at one side of the bench and set another at the other side for a witness stand. There was no jury because the plea was guilty. The lawyer they had assigned for Jess could do nothing except plead the youth of his client and the hard circumstances of his life. It did not take long, the brief series of witnesses to establish the facts. They called me to identify him and tell what I knew about him. They called Walton Eakins and had him repeat his story to put it in the court records. The defence lawyer was finishing his plea for a softening of sentence when there was a stirring in the room and one by one heads turned to stare at the outer doorway.

The father was there, filling the doorframe with his broad bulk in its black clothes. Dirt marks were on them as if he had literally wrestled with something on the ground. His hat was gone and his long hair flowed back unkempt. His beard was ragged and tangled and the cheeks above it were drawn as if he had not slept. But his voice rolled magnificently, searching into every corner of the room.

'Stop!' he said. 'You are trying the wrong man!'

He came forward and stood in front of the bench, the wooden pedestal we used for a trial bench. He looked up at Judge Cutler on the small raised platform behind it.

'Mine is the guilt,' he said. 'On my head let the punishment fall. My son has not yet attained his twenty and first birthday. He is still of me and to me and I am responsible for aught that he does. He was put into my keeping by God, to protect him and guard him from temptation and bring him safely to man's estate. My will was not strong enough to control him. The fault therefore is in me, in his father that gave him the sins of the flesh and then failed him. On me the judgement. I am here for it. I call upon you to let him depart and sin no more.'

Judge Cutler leaned forward. 'Mr Dutrow,' he said in his precise, careful manner, 'there is not a one of us here today does not feel for you. But the law is the law. We cannot go into the intangibles of human responsibilities you mention. Hereabout we hold that when a man reaches his eighteenth birthday he is a capable person, responsible for his own actions. Legally your son is not a minor. He must stand up to his own judgement.'

The father towered in his dirty black coat. He raised an arm and swept it up full length. His voice fairly thundered.

'Beware, agent of man!' he said. 'You would usurp the right of God Himself!'

Judge Cutler leaned forward a bit farther. His tone did not change. 'Mr Dutrow. You will watch quietly or I will have you removed from this room.'

The father stood in the silence and dwindled again within his dark clothes. He turned slowly and looked over the whole room and everyone in it. Someone in the front row moved and left a vacant seat and he went to it and sat down, and his head dropped forward until his beard was spread over his chest.

'Jess Dutrow,' Judge Cutler said, 'stand up and take this straight. Have you anything to say for yourself?'

He stood up, shaky on his feet, then steadying. The whipped-colt look was a permanent part of him now. His voice cracked and climbed.

'Yes,' he said. 'I did it and he can't take that away from me! Everything's true and I don't give a damn! Why don't you get this over with?'

'Very well,' Judge Cutler said. 'There is no dispute as to the pertinent facts. Their logic is plain. You put yourself outside the law when you committed the thefts. While you were still outside the law you shot and killed a peace officer in the performance of his duty and wounded another. You did not do this by accident or in defence of your life. Insofar as the law can recognize, you did this by deliberate intent. By the authority vested in me as a legally sworn judge of the people of this State I sentence you to be hanged tomorrow morning at ten by this courthouse clock.'

Most of us were not looking at Jess Dutrow. We were looking at the father. He sat motionless for a few seconds after Judge Cutler finished speaking. Then he roused in the chair and rose to his feet and walked steadily to the doorway and out, his head still low with the beard fanwise on his chest and his eyes lost and unseeable in their deep shadow-holes. I passed near him on the way home about an hour later and he was the same, walking steadily along, not slow, not fast, just steady and stubborn in his face. I called to him and he did not answer, did not even raise or turn his head.

The next morning I woke early. I lay quiet a moment trying to focus on what had wakened me. Then I heard it plain, the creaking of wagon wheels. I went to the door and looked out. In the brightening pinkish light of dawn I saw him going by on the other side of the creek. He had yoked the oxen to the big wagon and was pushing steadily along, leading them with the leather thong. I watched him going into the distance until I shivered in the chill morning air and I went back into the house and closed the door.

It was the middle of the afternoon when he returned, leading the oxen, and behind them on the wagon was the long rectangular box. I did not watch him. I simply looked towards his place every now and then. I had things to do and I was glad I had things to do.

I saw him stop the oxen by the cabin and go inside. Later I saw him standing outside the door, both arms thrust upward. I could not be sure, but I thought his head was moving and he was shouting at the sky. And later I saw him back in the shadow of the rock ledge digging the grave. And still later I saw him there digging the second grave.

That brought me up short. I stared across the distance and there was no mistaking what he was doing. I set the pitchfork against the barn and went down to the creek and across on the stones and straight to him. I had to shout twice, close beside him, before he heard me.

He turned his head towards me and at last he saw me. His face above and beneath the beard was drawn, the flesh collapsed on the bones. He looked like a man riven by some terrible torment. But his voice was low. There was no roll in it. It was low and mild.

'Yes, neighbour?' he said.

'Damn it, man,' I said, 'what are you doing?'

'This is my wife,' he said. His voice did not change, mild and matter-of-fact. 'She killed herself.' He drew a long breath and added gently, very gently: 'With my butchering knife.'

I stared at him and there was nothing I could say. At last: 'I'll do what I can. I'll go into town and report it. You won't have to bother with that.'

'If you wish,' he said. 'But that is all a foolishness. Man's justice is a mockery. But God's will prevail. He will give me time to finish this work. Then He will deal with me in His might.'

He withdrew within himself and turned back to his digging. I tried to speak to him again and he did not hear me. I went to the cabin and looked through the doorway and went away quickly to my place and saddled the grey and rode towards town. When I returned, the last shadows were merging into the dusk and the two graves were filled with two small wooden crosses by them and I saw him there on the ledge.

Three days he was there. And late in the night of the third day the rain began and the lightning streaked and the thunder rolled through the valley, and in the last hour before dawn I heard the deeper rolling rumble I had heard once before on a hunting trip when the whole face of a mountain moved and crashed irresistibly into a canyon below.

Standing on the porch in the first light of dawn, I saw the new broken outline of the cliff up and across the valley and the great slant jagged pile of stone and rubble below where the rock ledge had been.

We found him under the stones, lying crumpled and twisted near the big squarish rock with the wooden cross cracked and smashed beside him. What I remember is his face. The deep-sunk, sightless eyes were open and they and the whole face were peaceful. His God had not failed him. Out of the high heaven arching above had come the blast that gave him his judgement and his release.

In the Silence

Daylight was there at his eyes before it seemed he'd been asleep. Then he saw the big foot by the tarp-covered bedroll, and the foot moved to prod him again. 'Are you sleepin' all day?' demanded Angus Duncan.

Jimmy McDonald sat up and blinked at the big red-haired man who towered above him. Then he reached into the breast pocket of his heavy wool shirt and his chapped fingers brought out the silver brooch with its glinting purple jewel. He'd worn the brooch on his kilt when he left the hills of Scotland to come to Wyoming and learn the sheep business.

'Ah, that miserable glass and cheap silver,' Angus Duncan muttered. 'What kind of a never-grow-up are you when you must carry a trinket in your pocket?'

Jimmy couldn't answer. There was no way to put into words what he felt about the brooch. It meant home, the home he'd left to be under the guidance of this distant cousin of his father, the home he hadn't seen for two years. *Aye, that was a green and wonderful land across the ocean*, Jimmy thought, trying to stretch himself awake. *Not mean country like this with its late, cold spring and its mountain always there, frowning down on you.*

Jimmy shivered. Already he feared the mountain that towered above the campground almost as much as he feared Angus Duncan. Terrifying tales were told of those who lived too long alone on the mountains. 'In the silence', the herders called it, and sometimes, they said, a man too long in the silence was daft for the rest of his lifetime.

'Get up and stir the sheep,' Angus Duncan said now. 'Lambs should be at their breakfast before we start them up the mountain. Then we'll not have the ewes hiding from us among the rocks and brush to feed their young.'

Jimmy bent to pull on his boots. Finally he stood, tall for his fourteen years, and looked up at Angus Duncan. 'And what's my wages for sitting the summer alone on the mountain with your sheep?'

Angus Duncan's frosty blue eyes looked down on him from under the heavy red eyebrows and the stern mouth moved at the corners in what might have been a smile. 'Not content with grub and decent blankets anymore, eh? Well, I'll tell you—' Angus Duncan paused and looked at the mountain, its pines still black against the first morning light.

'Your summer's wages,' Angus Duncan said at last, 'will be the long-tailed lambs.'

A terrible empty ache began in Jimmy's stomach. 'But—they can die. The coyotes can kill them, and the wild range horses run over them, trampling them. I—I could work the whole summer and have nothing left to show for it.'

Angus Duncan grunted. 'Well said for a lad that's slow to grow up. You've spoken the truth, and the truth can be a hard thing to face. If you save the lambs, you'll beat the best herder's wages. If you lose them, you've yourself to reckon with.'

So Angus Duncan was laying out a hard lot for him, a mean job, and Jimmy recalled saying as much when he'd asked Angus Duncan to let him stay another month on the prairie with the other herders in their comfortable canvas-roofed wagons. 'Let me stay with them,' Jimmy had said. 'Let me move to high country when they do.'

Angus Duncan had laughed in his face. 'Does a boy learn sheep business by sitting with old men under shelter? Why, when I was ten years old, I trailed to the Big Horn Mountains ...'

Now, in the cold of this June morning, Jimmy went to where the sheep were bedded on the gentle slope that marked the beginning of the mountain. As he moved among them, they stirred like old grey stones coming suddenly to life and got up and stretched and nudged their sleeping lambs. These were the dock-tailed lambs, tails cut on the level prairie and with their legs already strong for the mountain trip.

He looked carefully for the swollen ewes, their bellies like grey barrels; the late lambs would run to sixty or seventy. *Aye*, he thought, *if I could keep only half I'd be a man of wealth.* But his lambs would be the late catches, born far from the familiar ground of the drop herd, prey to coyotes, early snowstorms that hit the mountain, and the salt-hungry horses that ran wild on the open range. Far from the world his lambs would be, brought to life near the sky, with no one to help him keep them from harm.

Jimmy's shoulders sagged as he moved towards the small fire with its smoke and fragrance of coffee. Angus Duncan silently handed him a tin plate, and they ate without speaking to each other, then loaded the packhorses and put saddles on the riding horses. On the packhorses were Jimmy's supplies for the summer—a tent, a small teepee, sacks of salt for the sheep, food and bedding.

It took five hours to get the sheep on the mountain, moving them slowly along the narrow paths between trees and rocks. But the dogs worked well. Jimmy and Angus walked, leading the horses, and it was hot before they nooned up in the high country. They rested while the sheep were quiet and in the afternoon moved them across the broad back of the mountain to where the snow-drifts still lay with their adjoining pools of water. Here the sheep would drink while there was water, and later use the springs that sometimes went dry by the end of summer.

'You'll set up your main tent here,' Angus Duncan said, 'and come back for food and to water the sheep. At night set up your teepee by the bed ground. I'll be back in a couple of weeks to move you on a bit. And one day, if you keep your wits about you, I'll let you be a camp mover instead of a herder.'

He'll make me no camp mover, when my long-tailed lambs are dead, Jimmy thought bitterly. *I'll be at the herding till I'm an old man if all the wages I get are long-tailed lambs.* And in anger he said loudly, 'Why do you come up here so soon—snow still on and nights like the middle of winter and not a soul to keep me company? I see no other sheep outfits up here.'

'The early sheep get the best grass and plenty of water,' Angus Duncan said. 'You'll have company by July—and the finest lambs.' Then Angus nodded to himself and rode away, leading the packhorses.

The silence of the mountain seemed to grow out of the grass and trees until it came to stand all around Jimmy. His heart beat loudly and sweat broke out on his body. He called to the sheep-dogs, his voice sounding strange and hollow, then went into the tent where the small stove, left from last year's early camp, had been set up. He put his bacon in a white sack and hung it high in a tree, for the flies wouldn't go high in the wind or the thin air. He stacked his canned goods in the corner and put other groceries in a box with a strong catch to keep it shut. Here he had his flour, salt, sugar, baking powder, soda, and sourdough mix.

The silence kept coming into the tent while he worked. And suddenly he felt an overwhelming desire for candy. But Angus Duncan wasn't one to feed his herders anything sweet. Plain food,

Angus Duncan always said, kept a man lean and strong and did no harm to his teeth.

Forget about teeth, Jimmy thought, finding a can of condensed milk and punching holes in it with his pocket knife. Then he got a tin cup and filled it with snow from a drift near the tent. He poured canned milk over the snow and covered this with sugar. He ate greedily. *Maybe the silence won't bother so much with a full belly.*

Jimmy set up a small teepee near where the sheep were gathering to bed down for the night. 'Don't bull the sheep about their bed ground,' Angus had cautioned. 'They know better than you where they'll sleep best.' He set his .22 rifle in the corner of the teepee. It was a single-shot and Angus Duncan had said, 'Enough gun for you, and see you don't ventilate a leg or foot with it. Nobody'll be around to bandage your bleeding.'

No, Jimmy thought, feeling cold, *there is nobody around.*

Two of the late lambs were born just before twilight and no sooner had the mothers licked their faces clean and the yellow saddles of membrane started to dry on their backs than the coyotes began howling.

Jimmy hurried to build fires around the bed ground, heaping up broken tree limbs and sagebrush, swinging the axe until his arms ached. When darkness came, he lighted the fires that circled the sheep. The thin, eerie *yip-yapping* of the coyotes rang out from time to time. Jimmy got his gun and walked around the bed ground. Once he saw coyotes at the edge of the firelight, their eyes glowing red, and he rushed toward them, the gun ready. They slipped away into the darkness.

He slept little that night, curled half in and half out of the teepee, the rifle close beside him. And it wasn't until the sheep nooned up that he felt free to lie down among the sagebrush and sleep deeply, the sun pouring over him.

He wakened to the thunder of horses' hooves and sat up blinking. He knew before he saw them come racing out of the trees into the open plateau that these were the wild range horses. Some had broken away from corrals and jumped fences and had run for years on open ranges. Now they wandered on to the mountain and were crazy in their need for salt, for there no salt sage grew.

While he screamed and groped for rocks to throw, they thundered past him, scattering the sheep. When they had gone, one of his new long-tailed lambs lay trampled and bloody and dead. He put out more salt for the sheep and vowed to shoot the range horses if they came back.

That night Jimmy again built fires to keep away the coyotes and from time to time paced around the bed ground. Five late lambs came during the night. The wind blew in from the north, spitting rain, but this he didn't fear as much as the coyotes or the range horses. There was shelter for the new lambs under the big sagebrush, and Angus Duncan had told him that sheared ewes died from cold more easily than lambs. From the moment of breath, the lamb was at home in the chill, Angus said, but the sheared ewe was without the cover she'd grown used to and couldn't stand much cold.

When the sheep nooned again, Jimmy was in need of sleep, but now the great silence of the mountain plagued him more than weariness. He got on his saddle horse and rode quickly to the rim of the mountain where he could look down on the prairie and see the white-roofed sheepwagons of other herders.

It was almost like talking to another person to see the wagons. He reached in his shirt pocket and took out the silver brooch he'd worn on his kilt in that long-ago time when he'd left Scotland. He turned the brooch in his hand, as though the faraway herders could see it shining. The silence roared in his ears.

At last he rode back to the big tent near the melting snow-drift. He unsaddled the horse and put hobbles on him. Then he noticed the big footprints where the ground was moist near the water hole. *He was not alone in the silence.*

Jimmy ran to the tent, shouting, 'Hey there!' But his voice seemed to bounce back at him from the canvas walls and he saw that the tent was empty. Disappointment filled him. It was surely a strange thing that a man would not stay and talk with him. In such a big, lonely country men didn't pass up the opportunity to talk to one another.

The silence of the mountain came pouring into the tent. He closed the tent flap as though to shut it out, but gigantic and real, the silence was there, all around him. *I must take hold of myself,* he thought. *I must look after the sheep.* And after a while the big silence ebbed out of the tent, much the way a tide draws back from the shore.

That night the coyotes were bad, circling the fringe of the lighted fires and making the sheep restless. Doggedly, Jimmy kept the fires going and walked around and around the ring of bedded sheep. Once he stopped and stared, for he was sure he had caught a glimpse of a man at the edge of the firelight. Then, it seemed, the man faded away. Queer little prickles ran up the back of Jimmy's neck. *Am I going daft?* he wondered.

At the end of ten days Jimmy was thin and hard, and his eyes, red from wind and sun, burned fiercely in his taut young face. Loneliness was in him, filling him like a bitter food he couldn't digest. Periodically the silence dropped over him in a smothering cloud and within it he'd stand, trembling and sweating. Once it was so terrifying he dropped to his knees and clutched the sage-brush to assure himself of his own reality.

There were now fourteen of the small long-tailed lambs. The bold, brassy blue sky mocked him, and out of it came the big eagles, plummeting down towards the new lambs. Sometimes he ran, shouting, to frighten them away. Sometimes he shot at them. Once, on the far side of the herd from where he stood, an eagle got a lamb, soared high with it, and dropped it. Returned and soared again and dropped it. By the time the eagle came in for the third catch, Jimmy was close enough to shoot at it. The eagle went away, but when Jimmy got to the lamb, the life had gone.

In these days that became more dream than reality, he ceased to hate Angus Duncan. He knew if Angus Duncan were to ride out of the aspen trees, now coming green in a quick mist, he'd run to the big man as though he were a lad again and running to his father.

On a late afternoon, when the wind was down and the shadows were long from the rocks and trees, a man came suddenly and stood by the big tent, a man with a gun in a bloody hand. There was something terrible and frightening about him; it breathed out of his dirty clothes, the blood on his hand, the mad light in his eyes.

He said clearly to Jimmy: 'I've come to take the long-tailed lambs. The coyotes will get them anyhow.'

Blinding anger came up in Jimmy. He tried to collect his wits, hold in check his rising terror. Then slowly he reached in his shirt pocket and brought out the silver brooch with the shiny purple stone that was the colour of heather in bloom. He let the treasure lie in the palm of his hand where the sunlight struck it from the west.

'You'll kill me to get my lambs,' Jimmy said quietly, turning the brooch to catch more sunlight so that it gleamed brighter than before.

'What's that in your fist?' the stranger asked.

'Silver and precious stone,' Jimmy replied. 'Worth more than all the band of sheep.' He looked into the stranger's eyes and saw them glitter.

'If you steal this,' Jimmy went on, 'a curse will be on you. This can't be killed for or stolen. But it can be bargained for.'

Now that he was making a story, he ceased to be afraid. It was like listening to his mother talk when the sea was rough and the fishing boats were in danger. Always his mother had told the children stories until the sea seemed a friend, and faith would come to them that their father would get home.

'I heard of a man who stole one of these jewels,' Jimmy said, 'killing a man to get it. Blindness struck him.' And he turned the silver brooch until the sun glinted on the glass, making a light that fell full in the stranger's eyes.

'But,' Jimmy went on, 'it can be bargained for, and no harm done. I'll bargain with you—this for you, if you leave my long-tailed lambs.' And he moved closer so the wild eyes could look more closely at the stone.

'I can take it—and the lambs.' The stranger spat on the ground.

'Aye.' Jimmy nodded. 'That is so. And you'll have to kill me, for I'll fight. It's for you to choose whether there's a curse on you or not.'

The stranger didn't speak.

Jimmy's hand tightened on the brooch. 'I'll never be the same without it,' he said, more to himself than to the stranger. 'It is giving something inside me away.'

Then the evil-smelling man moved close and held out the hand with the bloody fingers. 'I'll take it—and leave your sheep.'

When the brooch fell from his hand to the hand of the stranger, tears began to run down Jimmy's cheeks and the strength left his legs. He fell down to the ground and lay as one dead. When he awoke, it was dark, and he was cold and hungry. He jumped up, thinking only of the sheep, and ran to build fires and walk the bed ground. The dogs greeted him and licked his hands.

Two days later when Angus Duncan came riding up from the flat country, he looked sharply at Jimmy and said, 'Have you forgotten to eat, boy? What's happened to you?' And the big man got off his horse and put his hand gently on Jimmy's shoulder.

Jimmy talked slowly and carefully, telling his story of the stranger. Afterwards he waited for Angus Duncan to laugh at him or tease him. But Angus neither laughed nor spoke. He walked over to the dwindling water hole near the snowdrift that now was almost gone and looked at the ground. 'There is no track of a man here,' he said, 'but, of course, the sheep have been in to drink and trampled the earth.'

He came back to Jimmy and said, 'I brought you some sweets. Strange, how a man hungers for them on the mountain.' And he took a sack of candy and put it in Jimmy's hand.

Once Jimmy would have stood there and stuffed the candy in his mouth and eaten until the sack was empty. But now he only held the sack and said casually, 'I may have some tonight after my supper. Thank you.'

'In the silence,' Angus Duncan said, 'a man learns to be strong. And the silence is not only on the mountain, Jimmy. Somewhere— before he dies—every man must meet it and struggle with it on his own terms. In the silence we must face only ourselves.' Again Angus Duncan's hand touched the boy's shoulder. 'I see now you have done that.'

Jimmy's hand moved to his empty shirt pocket. *I could have lost the brooch, there at the edge of the mountain when I was looking to the prairie and the wagons of other herders*, he thought. *Still—*

'Well,' he said, 'you'll want to take a look at the sheep over there. I've lost only two lambs—one to the wild horses and another to the eagles.'

He walked with Angus Duncan towards the sheep. The light of later afternoon had given new shapes to everything, making even the grass look thicker and stronger. The silence was still there. But Jimmy smiled to himself, letting it move beside him as an old and familiar friend.

Acknowledgements

The editor wishes to thank the authors (or their agents or trustees) and publishers who have granted permission to reproduce the following copyright material:

'Mountain Skill, Mountain Luck' by Winfred Blevins, from *Give your Heart to the Hawks* (Futura).

'The Guns of William Longley' by Donald Hamilton. Reprinted by permission of Murray Pollinger.

'The Man Who Knew the Buckskin Kid' and 'Blanket Squaw' by Dorothy M. Johnson, from *The Hanging Tree* (André Deutsch and Ballantine Books). 'Blanket Squaw' © 1942 by the Curtis Publishing Co. © 1951, 1954, 1955, 1956, 1957, by Dorothy M. Johnson. Reprinted by permission of McIntosh and Otis, Inc.

'The Gift of Cochise' by Louis L'Amour, © 1952 by the Crowell-Collier Publishing Co. Reprinted from *War Party* by Louis L'Amour. © 1975 by Bantam Books, Inc. By permission of Bantam Books, Inc. Originally appeared in *Collier's*, July, 1952.

'Emmet Dutrow' by Jack Schaefer, from *The Big Range* (André Deutsch). ©1953 by the author. Reprinted by permission of the Harold Matson Co., Inc.

'In the Silence' by Peggy S. Curry. Reprinted by permission of the author and her agents, Lenniger Literary Agency, Inc. © 1969 by the author.